DEER DUPLICITY

PET WHISPERER P.I.
BOOK 15

MOLLY FITZ

ABOUT THIS BOOK

Lately I've been putting my P.I. business on the back burner in favor of planning my upcoming nuptials. But when my brand-new next-door neighbor turns up dead, I drop everything to investigate—especially since I had a clear motive for her murder and I don't plan on saying "I do" in jail.

The police say her death was an accident, but it doesn't seem so open and shut to me. A frightened buck may be the only one who knows what really happened, but I'm having a hard time getting him to stop running and start talking.

Another problem? Octo-Cat and I can't see eye-to-eye on how to tackle our newest investigation, which forces me to work with my other, less reliable animal sidekicks to get the job done. Can I not only prove foul play, but also solve the case?

1

My name is Angie Russo, and I live a strange life. Thanks to my charming fiancé and kooky nan, my life is full of love. It's also full of noise... so much noise.

I can talk to animals, and once they find that out, most don't want to shut up. It all started with Octo-Cat. He and I met at a will reading, back when I was still working a temp job as a paralegal. His owner had just passed, and I'd just had an unfortunate run-in with a busted coffeemaker. Put the two together and—bam—our odd friendship was born. The first thing we did together was solve the murder of his former owner, which took some doing since everyone else happily assumed the old lady had died of natural causes.

Once I'd officially adopted my tabby companion, I became the trustee for his rather generous trust fund, and the two of us moved into his former owner's old manor house. I brought my nan along, and she later adopted the most adorable pound puppy, a mostly black tricolor Chihuahua we call Paisley.

Somewhere along the way, our gang realized we had a knack for solving mysteries and started up an official business, which—much to my chagrin—has been dubbed Pet Whisperer P.I. The last thing I want is strangers knowing I can talk to animals, but luckily they all seem to think our moniker is a joke or some misguided publicity attempt.

Whatever the case, they're always happy once we get the job done. Admittedly, most of our cases are unpaid. And usually we're not even formally hired. Mysteries just fall into our laps, and well, what else are we going to do to fill our days?

I don't take kindly to being called an amateur sleuth, mind you. I have an official business with a registered LLC and everything. That makes me a professional, thank you very much.

My fiancé is the senior partner at a local law firm—the same one I used to work at. That place saw tons of turnover until Charles took his place at the top. Now things are nice and steady, and together the two of us make up the small-town Maine version of *Law and Order.*

The last prominent member of our quirky ensemble is our very own trash panda, Pringle. He's a sticky-fingered raccoon who lives in a treehouse out back. He likes cat food and Nerf guns, but he loves reality TV. Most of the time he causes more problems than he solves, but we love him anyway. Well, most of us do.

Even after more than a year together, I'm pretty sure I only register as "kind of like" on my cat's affection scale, and Pringle ranks much, much lower.

Me? I've got all the love I can handle between planning a wedding and getting to know the bio grandmother I recently reconnected with after a lifetime of not even knowing she existed. The best part? My Grandma Lyn can talk to animals too, and believe me you, we've talked about our shared talents until we were both blue in the face.

Nan still feels a little jealous, but she's working on it. I could meet a hundred long-lost relatives and would still never turn my back on the woman who raised me and in the process became my very best friend.

As much as I'm looking forward to tying the knot with Charles, a small part of me is dreading it too. I've lived with Nan almost my entire life—the whole thing excluding a brief period when I tried to establish independence in a crummy rental. Marrying Charles means I'll be moving in with him, and Nan has made it clear that we newlyweds should be granted our space when the time comes.

I guess for now I'll soak up every second with my funny, sunny grandmother. It's not like we'll be moving far away. In fact, I won't be moving at all. Nan has decided to buy her old house back from Charles—what a lucky turn of events that he bought her old place when she moved in with me at Octo-Cat's manor house—and Charles will move in here with me. It's a short drive and one we're all already used to making on the regular.

Things won't be so bad. Just different. I've already told Nan to expect me over for dinner at least five times per week, and I also plan to keep her room exactly as it is in case she ever decides to move back. She's not getting any younger, though I swear she's in better shape than me and will likely outlive us all... even Octo-Cat, who has nine lives to lose before he's through.

✳ ✳ ✳

Normally I wake up to the smell of Nan's fresh baked goods wafting from the kitchen. Today, however, a sharp pain on my chest lurched me from sleep.

"Confess or die!" Pringle shouted and sent Paisley scampering over my chest once more.

"Stop! You're scaring me!" the little Chihuahua yipped, tucking her tail tight beneath her as she ran.

"You're scaring us all, kiddo. That's what happens when you keep secrets from the fuzz." Now the raccoon was sitting firmly on my chest as if I were some kind of soapbox for his ridiculous speech. His claws were sharp, and it hurt.

"Pringle," I growled and shoved him off me. "You're not supposed to be in the house, and you're especially not supposed to be in my room."

"Sorry, toots. Didn't mean to wake ya, but you're harboring my main suspect, and that won't do." He shook a little black finger in the air. "There's no hiding from the long arm of the law!"

"But I don't even have arms!" Paisley cried. "I'm a dog. I only have legs!"

Pringle slapped his hand into his forehead and

sighed heavily. "Dick Tracy never had to deal with this, I can assure you."

I wasn't sure whether he was talking to me, himself, or an imaginary audience. Whatever the case, I was done with this whole thing. Ever since our resident raccoon developed a taste for old back-and-white gumshoe films, we'd all been short on rest. Lately, he turned everything into a case to be solved. Yesterday we were all treated to the case of "Why is the water bowl empty?" Admittedly, that one was pretty open and shut; Pringle spent more time recounting the glory of his victory than he did investigating.

"Go play somewhere else." I pulled the blanket over my head, praying that this time they might actually listen.

Paisley slipped under the comforter and licked the inside of my ear. "Mommy!" she squeaked so loud it sent me bolt upright. "Pringle says it's my fault there's a big truck outside. He said I've been feeding secrets to the Russians. But I don't even know who that is or why they're in such a hurry."

It was way, way too early for this. Unfortunately, past experience dictated there was no way I'd be getting back to sleep. Besides, poor Paisley had always been too easy of a target for Pringle. He would stay on her until I forcibly split the two of them up.

I groaned and swung my feet to the floor. "Pringle, you are not allowed in my bedroom. Not in the morning. Not ever. Understood?"

"Yeah, I understand. The cat and dog are allowed in, but just because I'm a raccoon..." He threw his arms up in the air. "That's profiling. Just because I've got a mask and rings on my tail. Frankly, I didn't take you for the type."

"Outdoor animals need to stay outdoors," I eked out between clenched teeth.

"Whoa, whoa, whoa, sweetheart. Do you even hear yourself?" Something lit in his eyes, and he laughed. "Oh, I get it. This isn't about me at all."

"It's not?"

"No, you're threatened by my investigative prowess. I get it. A failed P.I. like you? Of course you're threatened by a brilliant ingenue such as myself."

"Excuse me," I thundered, then chased the little bandit out of my tower, down two flights of stairs, and through the electronic pet door, which somehow he'd managed to hack once again.

Paisley ran behind me, barking the whole way.

"And stay out, you no-good doodoo head!" she ruffed before bolting through the pet door herself.

I pulled back the drapes to watch the two of them fly through the yard where, sure enough, an enormous moving truck stood idling in our driveway.

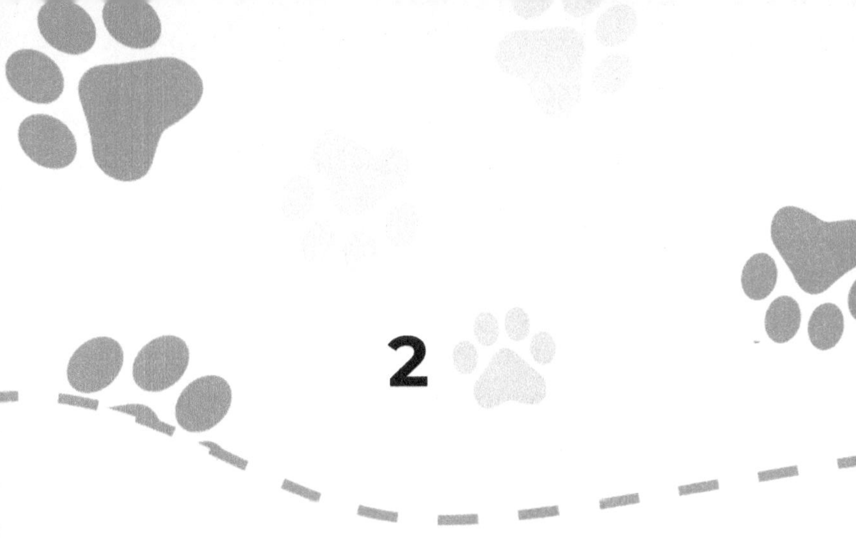

2

strode through the door and right up to that big truck, then motioned for the driver to roll down his window. When he did, he looked me over with an odd smile, making me realize I was still barefoot and in my oversized polka-dotted pajamas.

"Hi. Can I help you with something?" the driver asked, tipping his baseball cap cordially.

Suddenly I became very conscious of the fact that I wasn't wearing a bra and crossed my arms over my chest to preserve my decency as much as I could given the situation. "This is my driveway," I offered with a shy shrug.

He stared at me blankly, blinking a couple times in clear and utter confusion.

"I didn't order a moving truck," I added for clarity.

"Oh. Right. Sorry about that." The driver stopped speaking and frowned. After a bit of hesitation, he continued, "We're helping the old lady next door. My crew is running a bit late, so she sent me away and told me not to come back until we're all here and ready to clock in for the job. She also mentioned that she'd be reducing her payment."

"Confess!" Pringle screeched at the top of his lungs as he and Paisley darted beneath the truck, then ran back out again. Luckily it seemed like my companion didn't notice the rogue animals skittering about.

"Just how late is your crew?" I asked, trying to keep our conversation on topic despite the crazed antics taking place right in my front yard.

The driver glanced toward the digital clock on his dashboard. "Maybe seven minutes now. They had an early morning pack-up across town and agreed to meet me here to unload. That first job ran a few minutes over, but they're on their way now."

He sighed, and I inadvertently found myself doing the same.

"Sounds like your day is starting off a bit rough."

"I'll say." He dipped his head and sighed again just as Paisley and Pringle scampered off into the forest that lines our yard. Once again, he missed seeing them entirely. Still, I felt bad for the guy, having to wake up early just to wait.

"Can I bring you anything? Coffee? A muffin?"

The corners of his mouth lifted into an odd smile but then immediately gave way back into a frown. "That sounds divine, but I really shouldn't. I don't want to give the old biddy anything else to complain about."

Hmmm, this couldn't be good. My new neighbor had only just arrived and already she was leaving a sour taste in people's mouths. Then again, maybe she wasn't quite as bad as the mover was making her out to be. He could have fabricated his story to make his crew look better. Whatever the case, someone had finally moved into the vacant manor next door, and stopping by to welcome her would be the neighborly thing to do. Even if I was a bit nervous about it.

I said a quick goodbye to the driver, hoping the animals wouldn't resurface to bother the poor guy, then marched back inside to find Nan.

Normally she kept busy in the kitchen this time

of day, but today she was nowhere to be found. She had, however, left a handwritten note:

Out with Grant at Tulip Festival.
Back by Noon.

I flipped the notecard over and found a post-script scrawled on the back:

P.S. These are for the new neighbor. Tell her I'll come by to say hi later!

I swear, nothing happened in this town without my nan first knowing about it. A little heads-up about the new neighbor would have been nice, but at least she'd made up for it by putting together a lovely muffin basket.

I took a quick detour upstairs to make myself a bit more presentable, then grabbed Nan's latest batch of delectable baked goods by the wicker handle and headed for the door.

Octo-Cat lay snoozing in a sunspot by the entry-way. The tabby hadn't been there when I passed by a couple minutes ago, but now he was in such a deep sleep that he appeared dead to the world. *Best to let sleeping cats lie,* I reasoned, choosing not to disturb him until after I had some gossip to share about the new neighbor lady.

When I stepped out onto the porch, the big moving truck was still idling in my driveway but Pringle and Paisley had made themselves scarce. I hoped the wily raccoon wasn't being too hard on the poor little dog. Although past experience told me that would be just the case.

I'd go and find them after saying my quick hello next door and put an end to this game once and for all, even if it meant putting some kind of child lock setting on Pringle's streaming services. He'd eventually become obsessed with another film genre, but at least it would buy us some down time while he browsed.

One thing at a time, though.

As for my current task, the fastest way to the old Harlowe estate was via the woods that separate our lots, so I pushed my way through the thick canopy of trees, taking care not to upset my muffin basket.

When I emerged from the forest, I found an old woman with short white hair and a sour expression yelling into the cell phone she held out in front of her on speaker phone. I saw her profile as she paced her wide porch, but she didn't seem to notice me standing at the edge of her property with my basket of goodies.

"I already told you," she spat. "Wild dogs are roaming my property, and they're upsetting the local fauna. They already scared off a mother doe and her fawn when they tried to pay me a visit."

"Wild dogs?" the dispatcher on the other end responded skeptically over the speaker phone. "That's not a very common problem in Glendale, not since Pearl took over at the shelter."

"Are you suggesting I made this whole thing up?" the woman fumed.

The dispatcher immediately fell in line. "No, no. Of course not. Can you please describe them?"

Pringle came up beside me and placed a hand on my lower leg, making me cringe with fright. "Hey, toots. Whatcha got there?" he asked, gesturing toward the basket with his furry chin.

"Huge beasts," the neighbor continued as she motioned wildly with the hand that wasn't holding onto her phone. "One was black like a hellhound. The other had stripes."

I glanced down at Pringle and his big, fat striped tail. No. She couldn't possibly...

"Mommy!" Paisley let out a high-pitched bark, running across the lawn toward me and Pringle.

"There they are now!" the neighbor cried, finally looking up and spotting me.

I offered an uncomfortable wave and held the basket of baked goods out before me as a gesture of peace. "These are for you."

"Miss, Miss, are you still there?" the dispatcher asked after several moments of silence on the old woman's part. "Have you been hurt?"

She turned her back to me and continued. "Send someone immediately. My address is…"

I stood frozen to the spot in disbelief. What could Paisley and Pringle possibly have done to upset this woman so much in such a short period of time? And just whom had she called to issue her complaints? She wasn't even moved in yet for goodness' sake!

"Animal control is on the way," she turned to inform me with a steely gaze after finally hanging up the phone.

This startled me even more than Pringle's sudden appearance at my side. "Animal control? What? Why?"

"Seems you can't control your animals. Shame, but someone has to do it. They should be here within the next ten minutes. I suggest you take your two dogs and leave unless you want to have them taken to the pound… or worse." She let the implication linger between us.

"It's just one dog. A Chihuahua named Paisley." I bent down and snapped my fingers to call the dog to me. "She's really very sweet. I'm sorry if her playing disturbed you."

Paisley came running. Once she reached me, I shifted the muffins to one side and scooped the Chihuahua up with my free arm, tucking her into my armpit. "I'm your new neighbor, Angie. I live right next door with my nan. If you ever—"

"Can it, Angie. You only get one chance to make a first impression, and your hellhound already did it for you. I think it's best if we both just leave each other alone."

"But—"

She pointed toward the forest with a shaky finger. "Now go! Get off my property, or I'll call the police."

I briefly debated leaving the muffins, but you know what? She didn't deserve Nan's little bites of heaven, and I sure wouldn't mind scarfing down a few to help me forget this horrible start to the day.

Good riddance!

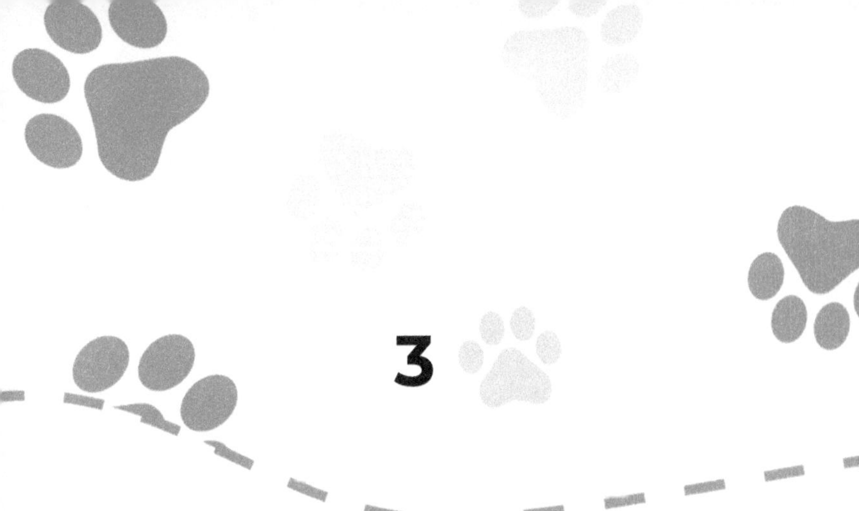

3

"Where were you?" Octo-Cat asked drolly as I strode back inside and all but slammed our heavy front door. "And hey, why the attitude? It isn't very becoming of you, Angela."

I stopped mid-stomp and turned to face my tabby where he sat idling on the coffee table. "I just met the new neighbor."

He flicked his tail and stared at me with large amber eyes that gave nothing away. "I take it things didn't go well."

"She was horrible. A monster!" I cried, throwing myself into the nearby armchair and sifting through the muffin basket until I found the one I wanted—a nice big cinnamon crumble.

I took a big bite right off the top, then continued speaking around my fresh mouthful of sweet and spicy mush. "She called Paisley a hellhound. And she called animal control on us! Wouldn't even let me say hi before she shooed me out of her yard." I swallowed my first bite and took another.

Octo-Cat pulled his ears back flat against his head until they almost seemed to disappear. "Has anyone ever told you that you eat very noisily and with far more saliva than necessary?"

I groaned. "Yes, *you*. And at least half a dozen times at that. Are you even listening to what I'm saying right now?"

"Believe me, I'm trying. It's just hard to make out your words over all the smacking and snarfing. I'm trying to lend a sympathetic ear, but you're being very rude, Angela." His tail began to wag wildly, suggesting that if I didn't give in to his demands, I may find myself on the receiving end of a serious hissy fit.

"Me? I'm not the rude one here, but never mind." I placed my partially eaten muffin on top of the others in the basket, then brushed off my hands and opened my mouth to show that it was now empty.

Octo-Cat nodded his approval. "You may proceed."

I repeated the whole thing again, becoming angrier and angrier as I did. Seriously, what was this new neighbor's deal? Did she just hate dogs, or did she hate all living things as a rule?

Octo-Cat held up a paw to silence my tirade. "You need to keep your voice down. Did you know cats can hear three times better than humans? Right now, you're little more than a noisy siren blaring right in my ear." He looked me up and down. "In fact you look like one too with that red face of yours. Did you wake up on the wrong side of the litter box today, or what?"

I grabbed the muffins again and hoisted myself from the chair. "Forget it. I'll go tell it to Paisley. Or Pringle. Or, hey, maybe the new neighbor isn't quite as bad as I thought, after all."

My cat said nothing as I marched away. His hot-and-cold attitude always kept me guessing, but I wasn't in the mood for games this morning. I needed a sympathetic ear and something worthwhile to distract me. Besides, I'd promised myself I would save Paisley from Pringle's pretend interrogation just as soon as I'd checked in next door.

Hmm. Now where could they be?

I stashed the muffin basket in the kitchen, keeping one in my hand to nourish me on my search, then headed back outside. Thankfully, the moving truck had now pulled away. Presumably they'd gone next door to finish their job of sticking me with the world's worst neighbor. *Bah.*

I wasn't often in a foul mood, partially because I hated who I became whenever rage flew through my veins. Maybe I could ask Nan to lead me on one of her guided meditations when she got back home. Or heck, maybe I'd hit the town and engage in a little retail therapy. True, considering my P.I. client load was light, my funds came directly from my cat's trust fund—but if he'd simply been willing to extend a sympathetic ear, I wouldn't need to find some other way to lift my spirits.

Yes, shopping. That would be a good way to keep myself busy today. Just as soon as I rescued that poor little dog of mine.

"Paisley!" I cried, trotting down the porch steps and sweeping my line of vision across the yard.

But she didn't come running. Didn't even bark in acknowledgment. Weird.

"Paisley!" I tried again, eyeing the forest for any sudden flash of movement.

When I still didn't receive any response, fear

began to claw at my quickly beating heart. The new neighbor hadn't hurt her, had she? Honestly, after our rude encounter, I wouldn't put it past her. Oh no.

I broke into a jog, rounding the house, calling out for Paisley at the top of my lungs.

"Yeesh. Will you quiet down already?" Pringle poked his head out of his tree house and stared down at me with shining black eyes. "Raccoons have hearing that's at least a thousand times better than humans. True fact. I heard it on the Kardashians. Anyway... you're giving me a headache, and you're interrupting my interrogation. Not a winning combo, toots."

"Mommy," Paisley whimpered softly from somewhere above me. What? *Noooo.*

"Pringle, did you...?" But I didn't even need to finish asking the question before I was tossing my muffin to the ground and launching myself up the ladder and into the trash panda's tree fort. Sure enough, the little dog sat cowering in a live trap. And every time she shook, the entire cage rattled in response.

"Pringle," I fumed, unable to tear my eyes away from the terrified pup. "How could you?"

He appeared unmoved by the whole thing as he settled himself comfortably in the window. "The dog wouldn't submit to questioning, so I had to bring her in."

"He said he would gag me if I answered you when you were calling, Mommy." Paisley spoke fast and in a higher pitch than usual. "I don't know what that means, but I was so afraid."

"Open the cage," I commanded between gritted teeth. "Open it right now."

"All right, all right. So dramatic. She's not hurt. See?" Pringle deftly unlatched the cage, allowing Paisley to bolt out straight into my arms.

"He dognapped me!" The little dog barked and whined, burrowing into me. "I've never been so afraid in my whole life, Mommy."

I stroked Paisley and cuddled her to my chest while glaring daggers at the raccoon. "Pringle, you're losing your TVs and your Nerf guns, and if I ever catch you inside my house again, I'll turn you into Davey Crockett wearable memorabilia."

Pringle brought a hand to his chest and gasped. "You wouldn't."

"Don't try me." Of course I would never hurt him or any animal, but he'd gone too far in kidnapping and trapping Paisley, all because of some imaginary role-playing game. I'd just about had it with this day already and was close to calling it off altogether. Would it really be that unforgivable if I went back to bed before even fully finishing my breakfast?

I tucked Paisley under my arm and then began to slowly descend the ladder. Halfway to the ground, a question popped into my mind and I retraced my steps. "Pringle? Where did you get that live trap?"

He shifted to his haunches and smiled at me with pointy teeth exposed. "Oh, I found it on the porch next door. It looked handy, so I swiped it."

A wave of anxiety crashed over me. "You stole this from our new neighbor?" If she found this thing on my property, she was going to be livid.

Pringle shrugged. "Steal is a harsh word. More like I borrowed it."

Now I was really torn. If that cruel woman actually managed to trap an animal, there's no telling what she might do to torment it. Then again, the last thing I wanted was to encourage Pringle's thieving ways.

"I'm coming back for it," I told him with a stern look before making my way back down the ladder.

I'd have to find someplace to hide it from the both of them. Yes, stealing was wrong, but animal cruelty was far, far worse.

Let's just hope I had a bit of time before she realized it was missing.

4

deposited Paisley in the second-floor bedroom she and Nan share, then closed the door so that Octo-Cat wouldn't come in and bother her. "Try to get some rest. I'll be back in a little while to check on you, and Nan will be home before you know it too."

"Mommy, can you stay with me until I fall asleep?" the little dog begged, and I didn't have the heart to say no.

I waited as she arranged herself on the pillow with the silk case that Nan kept on the bed especially for her doggie soulmate. Once she was cuddled into a tight little ball, I began to slowly stroke her fur, waiting for her breaths to come more slowly as sleep took her.

Soon I'd be getting married to Charles, and that simple act would change all our lives. Even though Paisley and I shared a close bond, she was actually Nan's dog, and she would be leaving with her when she moved out. My heart clenched as I realized just how much I would miss the little thing. Sure, we'd visit each other all the time, but it wouldn't be the same.

Even after Paisley dozed off, I could have sat there loving on her all day. But no, I had a live trap to hide. With a soft sigh, I let myself out of the room as quietly as I could so as not to disturb Paisley, then headed back outside.

Octo-Cat followed along without comment, which in itself was odd. He only spoke when I put my hand on the first rung of the ladder that led up to the treehouse.

"What are you doing?" he demanded with a cool, uninterested voice.

"Taking care of business," I mumbled as I focused on raising one hand over the other. The ladder wasn't built with humans in mind, and I worried that if I wasn't cautious enough, the whole thing might collapse on me.

Thankfully, I made it up without incident, grabbed the live trap and almost threw the darned thing down to the ground. Then my rational brain woke back up just in time to warn me that the noise might further attract the new neighbor's ire—and reveal the theft. I couldn't exactly blame the situation on the raccoon without sounding like a crazy person, so I did my best to climb down one-handed while holding tight to the cage with the other.

"Why was that up there?" my cat wanted to know when I'd finally made it to the ground. Of course he didn't offer to help, but at least he didn't criticize.

"Pringle stole it from the neighbor and then used it as a makeshift prison for Paisley," I explained, upset all over again as I recalled the horrific scene.

Octo-Cat shook his head. "Someone should really make Davey Crockett memorabilia out of him."

"That's what I said," I exclaimed, then realized I was really having a bad day if I was starting to sound like my cranky cat.

Octo-Cat exposed his claws and stretched into a complicated yoga pose. "Just say the word. As you know, cats are the most elite hunters in any biosphere."

I chose not to point out that his elite cousins

were all big cats, not house cats. I also didn't say that I was almost positive Pringle would win in a fight—what with his superior intellect and opposable thumbs.

"No more fights," I said instead as we rounded the house, side by side, just in time to see a white van with the county insignia pull into our driveway. Well, this couldn't be good.

A uniformed officer stepped out of the car and waved at me. "Good morning!" he called brightly as the day around me dimmed further.

"Hi," I called back, swallowing down a fresh lump of anxiety. I set the live trap down onto the grass and hurried my pace to meet him.

"What's that for?" the officer asked, motioning toward the live trap.

I stopped in my tracks, just a few paces away from him. "That? Oh, there was a raccoon in my house this morning. I thought I might be able to catch him and take him back outside."

"Is the wild animal still in your home, Miss?" He reached for the radio looped onto his belt, sending a cold bolt of fear straight through me.

"No, he's gone now," I insisted just as quickly as I could, then shrugged, attempting to appear casual. "This is just in case he comes back."

The officer frowned and dropped his hand from the radio. "Well, regardless of that situation. We received a complaint at animal control, and I was sent out to investigate."

"Yes, I was at the new neighbor's house when she called your office. I was trying to welcome her to the neighborhood. Lot of good that did." I laughed bitterly despite myself.

"Judging from the call we received, I don't think that's a very good idea." He shook his head and fixed his eyes on the driveway. "That new neighbor is quite the ornery sort. I'd steer clear if I were you."

"Duly noted. Anyway, how can I help you, officer?"

His eyes floated up to meet mine and a sad smile filled his face. "Listen, I'm an animal lover too, and I know how hard it is when you're in close quarters with someone who despises your pets. But the woman who called us was hysterical. It's our job to follow due diligence in cases like this."

I nodded along the whole time he was speaking, eager to send him on his way. "I understand. What do you need from me?"

"I'm going to need to check the tags and licenses for all your animals."

I tipped my head toward Octo-Cat who sat

silently watching the full exchange. "I don't have that for my cat, but I can show you vet records if that helps."

He eyed Octo-Cat for a moment before saying, "We really just need the paperwork for your two dogs."

"Who is this clown?" Octo-Cat meowed and lifted his leg over his head to groom his kitty bits. "Should I claw him up for you?"

"No," I shouted, eliciting a strange look from the animal control officer. "I mean, no, that's not right. I only have one dog. Actually it's my grandmother's. She lives with me too. Um, do you need to see her paperwork also?"

My attempt at a joke was completely rebuffed.

Now the previously sympathetic officer wore a scowl as he regarded me. "The caller was quite insistent that there were two."

"You can come look inside if it helps, but I only have one dog." I needed to try harder to play nice. It wasn't this guy's fault that my new neighbor was certifiable.

"Is this the striped one, or the large black..." He paused to check his notes. "Hellhound?"

I smiled despite myself. "Tell you what, I'll go

get her along with the paperwork and you can see for yourself."

When I returned with Paisley, the officer had a good long laugh. "Huge? She couldn't be more than five pounds soaking wet." He continued to laugh as he examined the Chihuahua's tags and looked over her paperwork.

"Everything's in order here, so I'll let you off with a warning today," he declared at last.

I let out a huge sigh of relief before realizing the news hadn't all been good. "A warning for what?"

"Your neighbor asked us to file trespassing charges," the officer revealed, then pressed his lips into a firm line.

"Are you serious? I just went over there to welcome her and offer some baked goods!"

"Not against you." He nodded toward Paisley in my arms. "*Her.* Technically, the charge would be dog at large."

"But that's ridiculous!" I argued, ready to march right over there and give that old crow a piece of my mind.

He sucked air in through his teeth, then shook his head again. "Technically your neighbor is in the right. Your dog shouldn't be on her property."

"Oh, okay." I looked down at the squirming pup

in my arms while I spoke. "We're just so used to that property being empty, but okay, I'll make sure Paisley doesn't venture back over onto her side of the woods from now on out."

"It's for the best." The officer reached forward to scratch Paisley between the ears. "I'm sorry you're dealing with this. Hopefully your new neighbor will cool down once she's settled in, but somehow I doubt it. Maybe consider a fence or a dog run?"

The whole thing was absurd. I hadn't had any luck, but maybe Nan could talk some sense into the woman next door. Surely this little squabble was something we could work out ourselves, right?

5

As it turns out, the squabble with the new neighbor next door was not, in fact, something we could settle ourselves.

That morning, Nan came back walking on clouds after touring the tulip festival with her beloved. When I told her about the contentious run-in with both the neighbor and with the animal control officer, she fired up her little red sports car and drove straight out to Misty Harbor to pick up some of our favorite lobster rolls from Little Dog Diner.

"The poor dear must be exhausted from her big move," she reasoned as she held up the white paper bag filled with delicious fare. "I bet she's famished

too. I'm sure it's nothing a little neighborly kind-
ness can't fix."

I tried to warn her off what I considered to be a
doomed plan, but she wouldn't have it.

Nan told me to be more compassionate, leashed
up Paisley, then disappeared next door while Octo-
Cat and I sat together at the dining room table and
got to work on our lobster rolls.

I was just licking my fingers clean when Nan
returned holding up a banged-up, crumpled-up bag
covered in dirty smudges.

"In all my life..." she huffed, slamming the bag
into the kitchen trash. "I've never met such a bitter,
such a detestable, evil old witch."

Paisley followed close behind with her tail
tucked between her legs and body cowering low to
the ground.

"That bad, huh?" I asked sympathetically.

"Worse," Nan said with a giant pout on her
wrinkled face.

I resisted the urge to say "told you so," and that
was that.

I did make a mental note to check the yellow
pages for some local fencing contractors and to set
up a quote or two. Other than that, there wasn't
much I or anyone else could do, other than hope

and pray the neighbor—whose name we still didn't even know—would see herself out of the neighborhood.

And that she'd do so sooner rather than later.

* * *

Nothing more happened for the rest of that day, which would later prove to be a rare and welcome break.

Because the very next morning, we received a second visit from animal control. This time a different officer stopped by with photos in hand as irrefutable proof that Paisley had crossed the invisible boundary that divided our two properties by at least three full inches.

Said boundary ran through the forest and was completely ensconced by trees. I didn't even know where our yard ended and the neighbor's began, but *she* did apparently. She'd even set up trail cameras to capture any movement along the border. I argued that my right to privacy had been violated, but apparently I was once again on the wrong side of the law with that one.

I tried to put it out of my mind, but the rest of that day was spoiled same as the one before.

The next day I didn't get any unwanted visitors, but I did receive a letter in the mail explaining that my refusal to keep track of my dog had led to a deer being scared off her property. I, for one, couldn't understand how this person could hate dogs so much while being seemingly desperate to make friends with the deer.

The note was handwritten but signed with only her address in lieu of a name. Even more off-putting was the fact that the envelope sported a stamp and postmark, meaning the bitter old woman had sent it through the post office rather than simply walking it over—or heaven forbid, trying to talk with us.

After that little surprise delivery, I drove straight to the pet store and invested in a hefty supply of pee pads. Paisley would just have to do her business inside until we managed to get that fence up. It wasn't ideal, but it was the best option we had available to us, all things considered.

Animal control came out for their third visit a couple days after I received the letter in the mail. This time they shared pictures of Octo-Cat helping himself to the bathroom on the neighbor's porch.

When I confronted him about it, my cat grinned wide, obviously pleased with himself. "Someone had to give that woman her due. She peed you off, so I peed on her porch. Justice."

Part of me was touched that the cat had decided to defend my honor, but a much larger part was upset he had created even more problems for us.

We sealed up the pet door then, because even with a fence, Octo-Cat could easily slip over or under to gain access next door. I'd already learned the hard way—and many times over at that—if I gave the tabby a direct order, he would go out of his way to do the opposite.

I prayed the fence contractors would be able to squeeze us in soon, but so far I was getting nowhere with any of the companies I'd contacted. They all claimed to have huge waiting lists now that the weather was warm. And somehow I doubted this was a job Nan and I could pull off on our own. Not with such a large property and not with such inten-sive labor required to get the job done right. Maybe Charles could find the time to help once he finished his current case. Whatever the matter, I was quickly becoming quite desperate.

* * *

Poor Paisley became notably depressed at having to spend her days indoors. Octo-Cat preferred being inside as a general rule, but the moment it stopped being his choice, he took to complaining loudly and doing so ceaselessly throughout the day. My home no longer felt like mine, thanks to the ridiculous expectations of our new neighbor.

"At least you'll be moving away in a month. Everything will be back the way you like it in your new house," I told Paisley to try to cheer her up. Of course that only reminded her that we would be splitting households after the wedding and sent her into an even greater state of despair.

My heart broke for the little dog, but honestly I didn't know what else I could do to help her. Especially since each time we'd encountered animal control, they reminded me that the new neighbor was technically within her rights, just that most people never minded about these things. I did receive a fine for Octo-Cat's little act of defiance, although I still don't understand what exactly I'd been charged with.

Like anyone could control the comings and goings of a cat!

* * *

After a full two days without incident, we received a visit from the police. A noise complaint that seemed to stem from Pringle watching television at too great a volume. I'd forgotten my threat to remove it from his treehouse after all the drama with the neighbor that took over the week. We were told to turn it down and be more mindful in the future. The thing is I couldn't hear his TV from our house, so how on earth had the neighbor heard it from hers?

* * *

Animal control came again the day after that. This time they were in search of the second dog the neighbor swore was patrolling her yard and upsetting her trash cans. Seriously, that woman really needed to have her eyes checked.

I helpfully let the officers investigate the entire house to prove we weren't hiding a secret second dog and gently suggested that maybe they charge the neighbor with something for wasting so much of their time.

Honestly, the more we tried, the worse it got.

Not even my sweet, lovable grandmother could charm her way into that woman's good graces.

Nan, of course, became absolutely incensed after this exchange and even went so far as to hire her Realtor friend to see if, for the right price, we might buy the house next door right out from under the neighbor. "I can sell my old home and move in next door. Then we'll be as close as close can be and also rid of the world's biggest nuisance."

But the transaction was a no go, and the next day we received another post-marked letter:

I know it was you.

Signed,

House #304

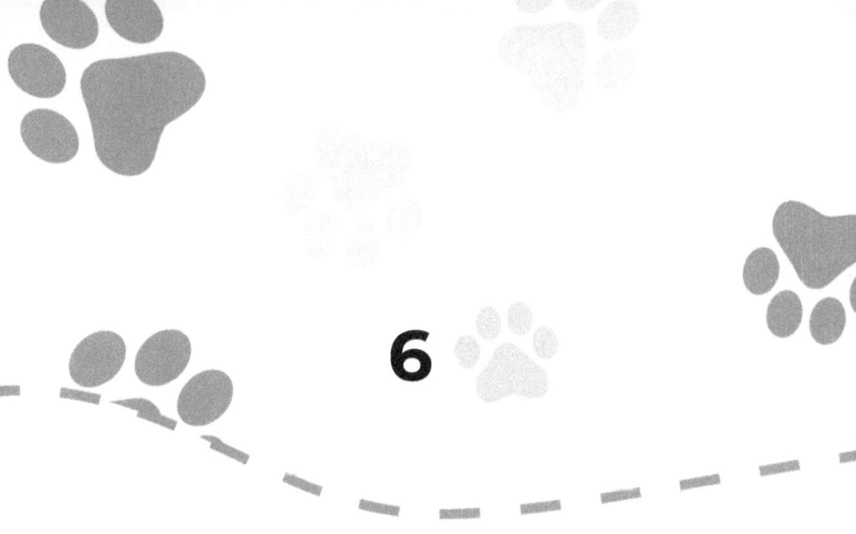

6

Over the course of the next week, we received visits from animal control and the police more days than not. At this point, I had half a mind to go pee on that cantankerous old woman's porch myself. If I was getting repeatedly punished for things I hadn't even done, I might as well actually get reprimanded for something I had.

It was fun to think about, but not something I'd ever do in real life. In fact, I didn't really do anything at all. Other than complain ad nauseum to Charles, effectively ruining what was supposed to a romantic evening.

I'd also asked my lawyer fiancé if I could reasonably sue her for harassment or emotional pain and suffering or literally anything that might stick and get her to leave us alone.

Charles said he would research precedents but that it probably wouldn't be worth the time and expense it would take to fight her in the courts. He also promised to help with our fencing project if I couldn't find a contractor by that weekend.

This, of course, was provided I survived until then, which at this point seemed like a pretty big expectation of myself.

I returned from my date that night both exhausted and angry with myself for letting this new rival take up residence beneath my skin. My agitation skyrocketed when I noted police lights flashing outside the neighbor's house.

Ugh. What could it possibly be now? I guessed I'd find out soon enough whenever the police came over to discuss the issue with me.

This neighbor was driving me out of my mind, and frankly I'd had quite enough. Perhaps that's why I was raring and ready to go when I spotted those police lights next-door.

Rather than wait for the officers to make their way over to my house, I was going to go over and find out what was going on for myself. And instead of traipsing through the woods, I decided to track back down my driveway and then march right up hers.

I wasn't usually a combative person, but the lady had never even given me a chance. Nan liked to say you caught more flies with honey than vinegar, but at this point, vinegar was the only thing I hadn't tried. Watching my morose animals laze about the house this past week with no reprieve in sight had filled me past overflowing with both spit and vinegar aplenty. I had to do something to defend my household and get our lives back on track. Otherwise, what kind of a pet owner would I be?

As I stormed up the driveway, I noticed that multiple cars had arrived on the scene along with a red-and-white ambulance, meaning whatever complaint the old witch had cooked up this time was a real doozy.

Thankfully, I spotted my old friend Officer Bouchard among the crowd. He'd saved my life when we first met. Maybe today he could save my sanity.

I waved and shouted a greeting, pushing myself into a jog to close the space between us. Strangely, I didn't spy my neighbor, even though she was typically right in the thick of whatever was happening.

"Listen," I told Bouchard, unable to hide my scowl. "Whatever complaint that horrible woman has cobbled together this time, I assure you it's completely off-base. She's done nothing but make my life miserable since she moved in, and she—"

Officer Bouchard placed a heavy hand on my shoulder, silencing me. "She's dead," he revealed with a soft wince.

I balked at this, unable to believe it. "Dead?" How could she be dead? Surely this was just another of her tricks. At this point I wouldn't put it past her to fake her death and then frame me for it.

"As a doornail," my friend in blue confirmed. "C'mon." He motioned for me to follow him around the house to where a little shed stood out back. The entire area was sectioned off with bright yellow crime scene tape.

Hmm. If this was a ruse, it was a mighty elaborate one.

"We still need to get an official report from the coroner, but we're reasonably sure this was an accidental death," he said, then pointed straight ahead. "Look."

I ventured closer to the shed and found my neighbor lying on the ground with her feet pointing straight up and a giant burlap bag covering her face and chest. Whatever was in that bag, it sure looked heavy.

"What happened?" I murmured, unable to tear my eyes away.

"Looks like this bag of deer feed fell off the top shelf when she wasn't expecting it, hit her clear on the head, and knocked her out." He pointed to the sharp metal frame of the shelf opposite. "She caught the edge there on her way down, sustaining a major head wound, then bled out before help could arrive."

Sure enough, a sticky puddle had flooded the small shed, staining the wooden floorboards red. The nauseating tang of iron filled the air, making me feel like I was going to be sick. If I had been home, would I have heard the crash? Would I have come to check in on her? No, I realized with bleak certainty, I wouldn't have even bothered to think twice.

I stepped back and turned away from the grisly scene, clutching a hand to my chest. Officer Bouchard followed me and offered his condolences, even though my words upon arriving at the scene should have made it clear I'd never been a fan of the old lady who lived next door.

"May I ask you a question?" I said, once I

managed to get the bile in my stomach to stop churning. When he nodded his assent, I continued, "What was her name? I never knew it." Somehow it seemed important that I know now.

He checked his notes and let out a chuff. "Looks like this was a Ms. Miller. Ms. Angela Miller."

We had the same name? How was that possible?

It's not as if Angie was an overly unique moniker, but still, the revelation that my sworn enemy had shared my name hit me in an odd way. Somehow, despite all the strife she'd caused me in the last two weeks, this simple revelation human-ized her. And suddenly I felt very sad.

What had happened to make this Angela's life so terrible? To make it easier for her to mail a letter next door than to simply stop by and talk? She must have been miserable and lonely—very, very lonely.

I don't know what I could have done differently, other than to be more patient, to give her a bit of time to open up to us. Maybe. I mean, if such a thing were even possible.

"Was it a quick death?" I asked, raising my hand to chew on a hangnail that had been bothering me all day.

"Probably not, I'm afraid, but it does appear she

was unconscious, so probably not too aware of the pain."

"Oh." I glanced back into the shed at the unlucky corpse, the heavy bag on top of her, and the pooled blood beneath her. Farther back, the shed was lined with a smattering of gardening tools, bags of fertilizer, and several more burlap sacks like the one that had knocked old Angela unconscious but much smaller. Why had she been reaching for the largest one when there were others she could have grabbed instead? Such a simple decision—choosing the big bag instead of the little one—had ended her life.

I couldn't even be happy that my problems were now over, not when it had cost someone their life. I was just about to thank the officer and head home to share the news with Nan and the pets when a terrible thrashing sound tore through the air followed by a panicked braying of some kind.

Officer Bouchard grabbed his gun and pointed it in the general direction of the sound, motioning for me to get behind him until he'd cleared whatever threat lay in wait.

But instead I dodged his attempts to shelter me and ran straight for the forest...

7

chased an odd pair of yellow streamers as they trailed deep into the woods. The police and paramedics stayed back, but they didn't know what was going on—I did.

"Wait," I called as I stepped carefully over a fallen branch but still snagged my foot anyhow. "Let me help you!"

But I couldn't keep up, and soon the object of my pursuit disappeared from view, taking the dancing yellow ribbons with him.

"What was that?" Officer Bouchard asked when I returned to the small crowd in my now-deceased neighbor's backyard. "And why in God's name would you run toward it?"

I leaned down and put a hand on each of my knees, woefully out of breath after the short burst of exercise. Nan would have my head if she knew how much I'd let myself go after we stopped our morning jogs.

"A big buck," I wheezed. "He wandered too close and got the crime scene tape tangled up in his antlers. The poor thing was scared out of his mind."

Bouchard tsked and shook his head. "A frightened animal is a dangerous one, which means you could have gotten yourself seriously injured back there. Think your nan would ever let me live it down if something happened to you on my watch?"

I rose to my full height and sighed. "You're right. I'm sorry." Apologizing was easier than explaining why I knew I'd be safe. Nan may have enjoyed blabbing about my secret abilities to all who would hear, but I preferred to keep mum.

Officer Bouchard gave me a friendly nudge on the shoulder. "Nothing bad came of it, but take a little better care with yourself, would you? We only have one Angie Russo in this town, and I'd kind of like to keep her."

I liked the officer, but I'd already seen more than I was comfortable seeing here. I'd happened upon more than one corpse in my day, but somehow Ms. Miller's irked me more than all the others combined. Maybe it's because we shared a name. Or maybe it was because of how I hated her, how I couldn't shake that this was somehow my fault.

Whatever the case, I just wanted to get home.

"I suppose I'll let you get back to it," I said with a tight smile, unable to summon an authentic one. "Please let me know if there's anything Nan or I can do to help with the investigation."

The policeman stretched both hands over his head and yawned. "There's no investigation. Seems like a pretty open and shut accidental death. Just as soon as we finish following procedure, we'll be ready to turn things over to the next of kin. Provided we can find some."

"Oh." I didn't know what to say to that. The whole thing was just very sad and unfortunate. "Well, good luck."

I hung my head and walked away, wondering if I'd somehow inadvertently contributed to the other Angie's untimely demise. I'd sure sent a lot of angry thoughts her way this past week. Maybe even wished she'd just disappear once and for all. But I never would have seriously wanted another human being to die just because she irritated me. Okay, maybe she did more than simply irritate me, but still… Of course, I knew it didn't help anyone now, me feeling sorry for myself, but I just couldn't help it.

I kept my gaze lowered to the ground as I traced my way back around the house, ready to head home, toss on my favorite PJs, and share the news with the others. If I'd been walking normally, I probably wouldn't have spotted the dusty tracks that led up to the basement egress window. I stopped abruptly, facing directly in toward the house. Maybe the old woman had locked herself out at some point and was looking for another way in, but somehow I doubted that. For starters, these tracks were enormous—far bigger than my own feet and definitely larger than the dainty ones I'd seen peeking out from the shed in the backyard. Someone—a man probably—had been spying on the neighbor. But why?

It couldn't have been the movers she'd mistreated. The rain we got a few days back would have already washed their prints away. No, whoever these belonged to had been here recently.

Animal control certainly came around frequently, but they had no reason to go peeping in her windows. Hmmm.

For a moment I wondered whether I should go share my findings with Officer Bouchard, but he had already told me Ms. Miller's death was an accident. Still, doubts continued to nag at me. If the new neighbor made enemies of me and Nan so quickly, how many other enemies might she have accrued over the years? Judging by the way she'd treated the moving company she hired, I'd guess that not many people had positive run-ins with the old woman, which made the string of suspects impossibly long.

I didn't even know where to begin. I knew nothing of Angela Miller's life before she moved to town and really knew nothing about it since. She'd only lived next door for two weeks, which meant if I were going to investigate, I'd be flying more or less blind.

No, I needed to tell the police what I'd noticed about the bootprints. They at least had a few more channels available to them, channels that weren't always open to novice investigators like myself.

Already past the point of mental exhaustion, I returned to the backyard and found Officer Bouchard chatting with one of the paramedics gathered at the scene.

"Forget something?" he asked with a knowing

glint in his eyes. He'd known me long enough to guess that the wheels in my head were now spinning wildly out of control.

A slight breeze blew past, sending a shiver straight through me. I wrapped my arms around my torso and said, "I found something odd. I was wondering if you could check it out."

He murmured something to the woman beside him, then followed me around the house.

"See." I pointed at the boot prints in front of the egress window. Now that he knew everything I did, I could take myself off the case. Ms. Miller had hated me. She wouldn't want me investigating her death anyway.

"What are we looking at here, Angie?" Officer Bouchard squinted, then squatted down to get a closer look.

"Bootprints facing in toward the window. Someone was either trying to look inside or trying to get inside." My eyes went wide as I voiced this revelation aloud.

But he seemed neither curious nor bothered. He simply shook his head and said, "Mmm. I don't think so."

Odd. Why was he so quick to dismiss my concerns? I knew Officer Bouchard well enough not to suspect foul play, but not even being willing to consider this new evidence? Definitely odd.

"What makes you so sure it's not a clue? I mean, really stop and think about it. Maybe her death wasn't really accidental after all." I bit my lip, waiting to see what he would offer in response.

My friend raised one foot and showed me the sole of his shoe. "The pattern matches, see?"

I studied the mix of straight lines and swirls stomped onto the ground, then compared the marks on the bottom of the officer's shoe. Sure enough, it was a match. Except for one small detail.

"But yours is much smaller than that pair," I pointed out, hoping it wouldn't offend him. Men were sometimes funny like that.

"They might not be mine exactly. But they could have been left by any of our team here. We all wear the same kind." He set his foot back down and furrowed his brow. "I'm afraid you're looking for smoke where there isn't any fire, Angie. I know it's scary, but I can assure you, what happened to your neighbor was nothing more than good old-fashioned bad luck."

"Well, if you're sure." I wrapped my arms around my torso again, needing that small bit of comfort. Whether or not Officer Bouchard agreed with me, something felt very wrong here.

He just shook his head and offered me a kindly smile. "I happen to be surer than sure. Nobody uses a bag of feed as a murder weapon. Can you imagine?"

Unfortunately, yes, I could.

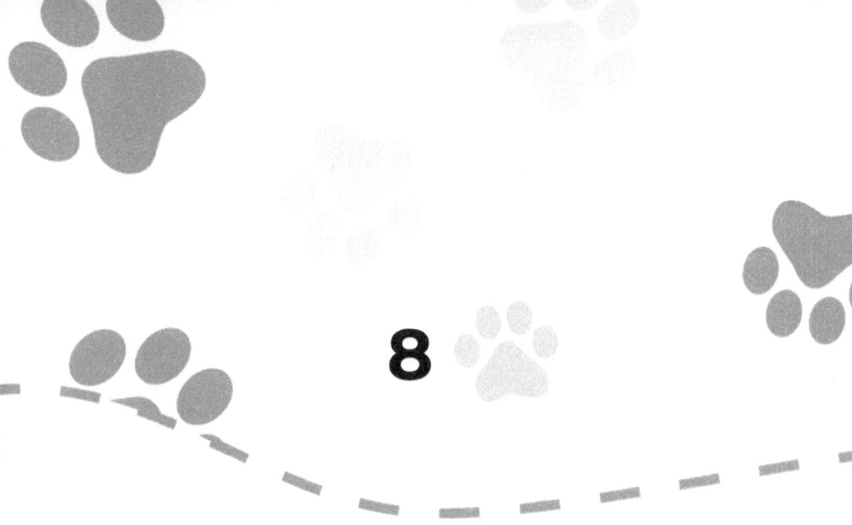

8

"Date night go that poorly?" Nan asked me when I appeared in the foyer after a sluggish walk home. "Don't tell me the wedding's off!"

"Everything's fine with me and Charles," I mumbled, sloughing off my shoes and leaning back against the door with a heavy sigh. "With the neighbor, not so much."

Nan was at my side in an instant. "Oh, what did that evil witch do now? I have half a mind to go over there and slap her silly. It's just our—"

"Nan," I interrupted, then took a deep stuttering breath before revealing the harsh truth. "She's dead."

A strangled noise escaped Nan's throat, telling

me she now felt quite similar to how I had at receiving the news.

Octo-Cat came trotting gaily down the stairs, his tail held high with a jaunty twist. "Well, that's one less problem in our lives. Will you break out the catnip or shall I?"

I turned on him so fast, I almost lost my footing and had to reach out for the banister to steady myself. "Octavius Maxwell Ricardo Edmund Frederick Fulton Russo, soon-to-be Longfellow too, how dare you talk like that? A woman is dead!"

He plopped down on the bottom stair and regarded me stonily. "One, I am not taking UpChuck's name. Try that again, and I will be removing the Russo from my formal title as well." He paused so long, I almost spoke again, but I also knew better than to interrupt a cat mid-list.

"Two, that hag made our life miserable," he continued after nearly a full minute stretched in silence. "You and Nan can act all lovey-dovey if you want, but I know the truth. You hated her, and you're glad she's gone."

"That's it!" He had me in a proper rage now. I was so angry that I was shaking. How could he act so cavalier? This was beyond the pale even for him.

"Go to your room and think about what you've done."

Octo-Cat hung his head and laughed mirthlessly. "My house, my rules. Or have you forgotten that all of this is mine?" Another long pause punctuated this rhetorical. "I get that you're having some trouble processing this all right now, but there's no reason to take it out on me. Now if you'll please, I need my Evian topped off."

"I take it he just said something nasty," Nan mused from her place beside me. Sometimes I really envied her for not being able to hear the cat's constant stream of commentary on our lives.

I scoffed, continuing to stare daggers at the bad kitty before me. "When does he ever say anything else?"

He shifted his weight from side to side, looking bored with the whole thing. "You humans are weakened by your sense of moral purpose sometimes. A cat, being the superior intellectual creature he is, can see the world for exactly what it is. Humans always like to complain that life isn't fair, but it seems to me that justice was served. The lady next door simply got what was coming for her. Got it? Now don't at me." Having said his piece, he lifted his tail up high and sauntered away while I watched in silence.

"I told you to stay off Twitter!" I yelled after him. It was definitely not to my benefit that I'd taught Octo-Cat how to download apps on his iPad. I doubt he was able to type out his own tweets, but it was bad enough he'd begun adopting the lingo. If he and Pringle ever put their heads together—and realized the cat had the tech while the raccoon had the agile fingers—they could cause some real damage on the interweb.

Unfortunately, this wasn't my most pressing problem at the moment. "The police said it was an accident," I told Nan, speaking hardly above a whisper lest Octo-Cat overhear and add more of his garish commentary.

Nan raised an eyebrow at me. "But you're not so sure."

"You know me too well," I said with a sigh when usually these words would be accompanied by a laugh.

"I found large footprints in front of the basement window. Someone was looking in. Possibly planning a break-in."

"Do you think that maybe—?"

"Angela," my cat yowled, interrupting quite

rudely. "Evian! A cat could die waiting, and we both know I'm already light on my remaining lives. I'd hate to lose one of the precious few I have left to dehydration."

I groaned and threw up my hands. "Be right back. His royal pain in the butt needs me."

"I heard that!" he mewled in protest.

"Good!" Sometimes it really felt as if I was the mother of the world's most unruly teenager. At least when Charles and I had children one day, I'd be ready for their worst.

I stomped into the kitchen. Octo-Cat waited in cold silence as I hand-washed his favorite china teacup, fetched a fresh bottle of Evian from the pantry, and poured. Next time he'd be getting toilet water, the little scoundrel.

When I left the kitchen, I rejoined Nan, who had moved to the living room and was now sitting with a sniffling Paisley on top of her lap.

"I take it you overheard what happened to the new neighbor?" I asked the little dog with a curious glance.

She looked up at me with huge, glistening eyes. "Is she dead because of me?"

"No!" I answered emphatically. "Absolutely not."

Paisley shook and whimpered. "Maybe she got scared to death when she saw me."

"She got knocked out by a huge bag of feed, hit her head, and then bled to death," I stated bluntly. We all liked to pretend that Paisley wasn't a teeny-tiny thing, mostly because she saw herself as a big, scary dog—the way all chihuahuas do. But I couldn't let her go so far as to blame herself for something that had absolutely nothing to do with her.

"Ouch. That doesn't sound very nice," Nan interjected. I'd shared the cause of death for Paisley's benefit, but this was her first time hearing it too.

"I'm sure it wasn't." I shrugged, needing to be strong for the two of them even though inside I was still reeling.

"Mommy, what's hell?" the pup asked in that sweet, sing-song voice of hers.

Of course, Octo-Cat chose this precise moment to make his grand re-entrance on the scene. "It's where that old—"

"Octo-Cat, shush!" I yelled before he could complete that thought aloud. Narrowing in on the frightened dog, I murmured softly, "Why are you asking about hell, Paisley?"

"The lady. She called me a hellhound. I know what hound means, but not hell. So what is it, Mommy?"

"Oh, dear." Nan scratched Paisley's head while wearing a worried expression. "I didn't want to bother the animals with religion, but if they can talk, I guess they can also understand. Was this an oversight on my part? Is it time we took Octo-Cat and Paisley to church?"

"Touch me, and you're dead," Octo-Cat growled before running off.

"Mommy?" Paisley asked pointedly again. "Are you going to tell me about hell?"

Honestly I didn't know which of my companions to address first. We had a possible murder on our hands, and the shock of it had worn on us all. Now hardly seemed like the proper time to ponder such existential questions as they pertained to our house pets.

I moved to sit beside Nan on the loveseat and placed one hand on her shoulder while using the other to scratch Paisley's head. "We'll talk about this some other time, okay?" I told them both, hoping that would be enough for now. I already worried about the state of my cat's soul after the remarks he'd made, and I just didn't have the energy to follow this particular train all the way to the station.

Not now. Probably not ever.

I hardly had the energy to consider what happened to old Ms. Miller, but maybe after a good night's rest I'd be able to see things a bit more clearly.

9

My sleep came long and troubled that night. I was surprised when I awoke late in the morning the following day; normally the animals rousted me from my sleep hours earlier.

I tiptoed downstairs, finding only a quiet house to greet me. Nan and Paisley must have gone out somewhere, but where was my cat?

Feeling some minor hesitation, I unlocked the pet door. There was no sense in keeping the animals cooped up inside now that Ms. Miller was no longer around to issue complaints for every minor perceived infraction. Still, it felt weird, moving on so quickly. For the last two weeks, the neighbor's complaints had dictated so much of our lives, and now they just didn't matter anymore.

"Octavius?" I called into the seemingly empty lower level of our home.

When I was met only with silence, I moved to the kitchen to see what Nan had left for my breakfast.

There I found a note tucked under the edge of a blue ceramic plate—and on top of that plate, three fresh-baked vanilla bean scones. I grabbed a pasty hungrily, sweeping my eyes over the note as I chewed.

Flash mob in the park. Took Paisley.

Ah, that was right. Nan had started taking hip-hop dance lessons a few months back and had been over the moon when their class was invited to participate in a sneak dance number. It didn't exactly seem like Paisley's type of thing, but I imagined she'd be standing on the sidelines with Grant as they both lovingly watched Nan twerk and grind.

I glanced down at my baggy T-shirt and shorts with a snort. My grandmother was so much cooler than me. That probably should have bothered me, but it didn't. Not when I had so much else on my mind.

I still hadn't found my cat, so I decided to mount a search. I grabbed a bag of treats from the pantry and made the crinkling noise he adored, hoping it would draw him to me as I made my way through the house.

He wasn't downstairs, nor was he in my bedroom or even curled up in his own. I finally found him in the office, tucked away under the desk where a dark shadow kept him mostly hidden from view.

"Those for me?" he mumbled and crept toward me on four shaky feet to demand sustenance.

I shook three out of the bag and placed them flat on the palm of my hand. "What are you doing in here?"

"Couldn't sleep," he snuffled despite the fact he was still chewing—and the fact that he'd given me guff for doing the very same thing just last week. He must have been really out of it to do such a thing.

"Nightmares?" I offered with a supportive frown.

He shook his head.

"Regret?" I tried. My frown deepened as I recalled our conversation last night.

Octo-Cat stopped munching and met me with odd eyes. "Why would I ever feel regret? I'm a cat, remember?"

"Yes, I know you're a cat, but you were also kind of a brat when you heard the news about that poor woman next door."

He laughed bitterly, then began to choke, then coughed up a bit of food, then continued, "A brat? How dare you call me such a detestable name? And how dare you for even one second accuse me of being fallible? Besides, are you sure the old woman is even dead?"

"Of course I'm sure. I saw the body." How could he even be questioning this? We'd both seen enough bodies in our day to recognize the strange waxiness of a dead person versus a living one.

"Not dead, pah. Then how do you explain the lights that were flashing over there late last night making it nigh impossible for me to catch any shut-eye?"

This caught me off guard. "Lights? It must have been the police."

Octo-Cat snarled but knew better than to take a swipe at me while I was feeding him. "Do you think

I'm a moron? I know what police lights look like, and these weren't them. They were much smaller... More treats."

"What do you say?" Sometimes I wished I could snarl, but the best I could settle for in response to his lack of decorum was a frustrated groan.

"Now." His tail flicked and swished.

I groaned again and shook more of the tiny meat bites into my hand for him to nosh on. "You're welcome," I added pointedly.

A low growl rumbled in his throat. "Torches, I think they're called," my cat then offered before digging back in.

I blinked back my surprise, immediately picturing an angry mob wielding pitchforks and torches. But that didn't make any sense, unless...

"Hey, Octo-Cat. What have you been watching on TV lately?" I asked, knowing how impressionable and how theatric he could be. His viewing habits could very well tell me all I needed to decode his slang now.

His ears perked up at this. "Why, Angela, I'm so glad you asked. Usually you don't show interest in my viewing habits, considering my taste is so much more highbrow than your preferred media consumption."

"Uh-huh." I didn't have it in me to argue with him now, not when he seemed to have some information that I needed.

Octo-Cat straightened and met me with large, glowing eyes. "Lately I've found myself rather engrossed with this cheeky little drama set in London. The premise is—"

"Got it. You've gone BBC on me."

"Yes, but what's that got to—"

"You spend time on Twitter, you pick up that lingo. You spend time in front of BBC, you adopt Britishisms into your everyday speech. It makes perfect sense now."

He narrowed his eyes, giving his fuzzy countenance a sinister effect. "The Queen's English is the correct English."

I shook my finger at him. "Don't even get me started on that whole argument, or the fact that you've never once stepped paw outside of the US. My point is you're saying torches, but you mean flashlights."

"Beg pardon?" Now that it had been pointed out, he was really playing up this whole British angle—God help me.

"Wait there," I instructed, sprinkling a few more

treats out onto the ground to assure he would do just that.

I grabbed the flashlight we kept in the hall closet in case of emergencies, then clicked it on before returning to my erstwhile feline companion. "Is this what you saw?" I asked, sweeping the tiny spotlight around the room.

"Yes, that's a torch, Angela. Brilliant. Very nicely done." He rolled his eyes in derision. The smarmy part of me wanted to offer him a spot of tea and ask after his mum, but I had more important things to focus on than my cat's penchant for theatrics.

"What time did you see the lights? Are you sure they were coming from next door?" I pressed.

"Very late. Or rather, quite early. Maybe two, three o'clock. And they definitely started next door, but then they moved to the woods."

"Did they ever come to our yard?" I asked, a fresh jolt of fear striking me dead in the heart. The neighbor and I shared a name. What if whoever was out there had meant to come for me, but somehow got their wires crossed? And what if they were still coming?

A woman was dead, and still the vultures were

out there picking at the crime scene. Who were they, and what could they possibly want?'

Octo-Cat finished devouring his treats, then began to groom himself as he liked to do post-meal. He paused thoughtfully after several strokes of his tongue across his tail. "I must say, my dear Angela, it seems that something odd is afoot."

"Why yes, Octo-Cat. I couldn't have said it better myself." I smiled at this. While he was being rather annoying today, at least I had his interest. That meant he would help me, despite his lack of sleep the night before. And as they say, two heads are better than one, even when one of those heads is adorned with whiskers.

10

After opening a fresh can of Octo-Cat's preferred cat pate and pouring him a teacup of Evian, I spent the next ten minutes waiting while he took his time with breakfast. In the meantime, I polished off all three scones and made a mental note to have my wedding dress refitted just in case all this stress eating was having an effect on my waistline.

Upon finishing his meal, Octo-Cat then had to tend to his morning ministrations. The small amount of grooming he'd managed while we talked in the office was nowhere near enough to satisfy his habitual self-care.

As he tended to his hygiene, I composed a lengthy text to Charles to catch him up on everything that had gone down since I saw him for our date last night. The poor guy had been working overtime—and then some—to ensure he'd be able to take a full two weeks off for our honeymoon. I hated to bother him with my problems, but I also knew I'd never hear the end of it if I failed to inform him of something so major going on in my life.

I explained the situation as succinctly as I could, finished my message, and hit send.

Less than a minute later, I received notification of his reply. Just enough of it popped up on screen to tell me I shouldn't open it to read the full thing— at least not yet.

Whatever you do, don't disturb the scene to—

Yeah, nope. If I opened that, he'd know I saw his message and then consciously chose to ignore it. Charles knew me well enough by now to know exactly what I planned to do, which is why he was trying to warn me off it.

Maybe if I called the police with this new intel, they'd head over to investigate, but that wasn't a chance I could afford to take. Not when they'd dismissed my concerns about the shoeprints so quickly yesterday.

Besides, I just had a hunch that Ms. Miller's death wasn't as open and shut as it seemed. Something strange was going on over there, and I intended to figure out what.

"Are you ready, Angela?" Octo-Cat asked after one last lap at his paw. Like Charles, my cat also knew exactly what I planned to do. That's part of the reason we made such good partners—at least when we weren't bickering and nitpicking each other.

I nodded. "Let's go check it out."

"Tut, tut. Cheerio." This whole English act was quickly draining on me. I needed Octo-Cat to be wearing his detective hat, not one that belonged to a misguided thespian. Luckily, I knew just how I could shut this down while making it seem like the whole thing had been his idea.

"Cheerio, funny. You know, that reminds me of the time Pringle knighted himself and decided to vanquish forest monsters in the name of the queen. What was it he would say? Oh, right." I put on my most horrible impression of an accent combined with my most horrible impersonation of Pringle to seal the deal. "Pip, pip, cheerio, my good lad."

I glanced down to Octo-Cat and found his face filled with derision.

"Gag. Could we not talk about the trash panda?" he begged, reverting to his normal East Coast polish. "I'd rather die choking on a hairball, thank you very much."

I smiled to myself as we exited the house side by side and trekked through the woods.

"So remind me again why we're investigating?" the tabby asked as our feet crunched over fallen leaves that had been left to decay since last autumn. We couldn't exactly rake up the entire forest.

"Because the neighbor is dead, and it might have been murder," I reminded him, surprised he had forgotten our mission so quickly today.

"Right, but we hated her. Also aren't you busy enough planning your wedding?" He stopped to sniff the base of an old tree, and I waited.

"Hate is such a strong word," I reasoned.

He smirked. "But it's the correct word, isn't it?"

I groaned in acknowledgment, unable to address his pointed comment with actual words. "I am busy with the wedding, but I can't just let a murder go unsolved." The truth was I'd already finished the hardest part of planning my nuptials —figuring out the guest list and sending out formal invitations. As it turns out, I know a lot of people, making the rest of it far easier by comparison.

"Why not? The police do it all the time," he commented rudely, once again making me wonder how much time my cat spent browsing Twitter.

Just like I hadn't wanted to talk religion with the pets, I also didn't want to get into something so political. "Don't talk like that. The police do their best, but not every case is solvable." Debating Octo-Cat never went well, no matter what the topic. He didn't consider facts valid unless they proved the point he already wanted to make.

He left the strange-smelling tree behind and began moving forward again, leading us both through the woods. "So what makes you think this one is? Solvable, I mean?"

I was getting nowhere by assuming my cat had something akin to a human conscience. At the end of the day, he was a coldly logical being who would always put himself first, no matter the circumstance. As a result of our years together, I'd learned that my cat had two tragic flaws—pride and curiosity. Right now he was tagging along because of the latter, but the moment he lost interest, I'd be left on my own again. Unless... I needed to find a way to channel his pride to make sure he saw this through to the end.

"I don't know if this one is solvable," I admitted with a practiced look of consternation. "But I do know we have a much better chance of solving it if we work together. You know I'm nothing without you, Octavius."

He nodded along, completely unaware of how already I was playing him like a fiddle. "This is true. You need me, Angela. You've always needed me."

"I do," I agreed emphatically. "And what's more, this crime happened right next door. What if the killer comes back and tries to break into our house next... tries to break into YOUR house?"

Octo-Cat reared back and thrashed his front paws in the air like a tiny, unskilled ninja. "Then he'll have another thing coming when he meets the business end of these claws. Nobody comes into my house without my say so."

Now I was the one nodding like a broken bobble head as I brought my final argument home. "I don't know for sure a murder happened. That's why I need you to come check it out and make sense of things for me. We need to protect our home, and I'm not confident I can do that without your help, Octavius."

"Well, of course you need my help, dear Angela. Why didn't you just say so in the first place?"

I shrugged nonchalantly while inwardly beaming with confidence in a job well done. I'd played to my cat's hubris so many times, it was no longer difficult for me to put my pride aside to bolster his own. He was the one who had seen the flashlights last night, and he was the one who could get in and out easily without being spotted or leaving any fingerprints behind. And as much as I liked to puzzle out the clues, Octo-Cat was the one with a truly obsessive mind. Once he gave head-space to a case, he didn't stop until he found the answers he was looking for.

Maybe the new neighbor hadn't been murdered, but I couldn't risk the chance that she had been. Not when this had all gone down so close to home. The police had been quick to rule Angela Miller's death an accident, but I still needed more proof.

11

Octo-Cat and I finished our trek through the woods and approached the neighbor's large front porch. Potted plants flanked the steps on either side, and vibrant flowers dripped down from hanging baskets, creating a welcoming entrance so at odds with how the woman herself had treated visitors. It felt eerie to be in her space when she had so clearly not wanted us here.

"Okay, where do we begin?" I asked my feline companion as I took stock of the porch and yard. The police had already cleared out, which meant we were alone.

"You could go to the door. See if it's unlocked," Octo-Cat suggested in a snooty tone that seemed to imply I should have been able to think of that on my own.

I flexed my fingers demonstratively. "It would leave prints."

Octo-Cat scoffed. "Since when do you care about that? You leave DNA evidence behind all the time."

"Yes, but normally I don't have a motive that could peg me for the murder." I hadn't really considered this until now, but suddenly it became a very real concern. My troubles with the neighbor were well documented. What was I doing trying to prove foul play when the police were happy to leave it alone?

"The police said it wasn't murder," Octo-Cat reminded me even though I was already thinking the exact same thing. It was probably time to admit that I had quite a bit in common with my cat. I was too curious to leave this alone, even though I probably should have. I was curious, but I could still be careful.

"They say that now, but what if they change their tune?" I shrugged. "I'd rather not incriminate myself, if I can help it."

Octo-Cat jumped up on the porch railing and

paced back and forth. "Fine. Then what do you want to do?"

I thought for a moment. "Let's head around back. I'll show you the shed where I saw the body."

That was all I needed to say for him to leap down and take off running toward the back of the house far ahead of me, forcing me to do a light jog to catch up.

"It smells awful," he said as soon as we made it to our target location.

"Well, there was a lot of blood." I sniffed at the air but couldn't pick up anything unusual beyond the acerbic taint of chemical cleaners hanging in the air.

"No, that's not the smell. Blood, I don't mind. I am a carnivore, you know. For me, blood is a bit like a delicious gravy."

I cringed at the thought and briefly reconsidered becoming a vegetarian, as I so often had since gaining my strange gift. "Right, then what do you smell?"

Octo-Cat shuddered and shook out his fur. "No clue what it is. Only know I don't like it." Well, this was getting us nowhere fast.

"It's not exactly helpful when you—"

"Angela, silence." Octo-Cat lifted his head, ears alert and body rigid.

"What?" I paused and glanced around in a panic but saw nothing out of the ordinary.

But Octo-Cat remained tense and frozen. "Shhhh, there's something out there," he insisted.

I turned in the direction he was looking, back toward the forest. I couldn't see or hear anything. "What is it? Is it something dangerous?" I whispered.

"Will you just keep quiet already?" my cat bellowed, forgetting his own call for silence.

At last, a strange, garbled noise rose from the edge of the forest, and a flash of yellow caught my eye. "I... I... I... I am being as qu-qu-quiet as I can!" an unfamiliar voice declared before its speaker had moved fully into view.

"It's you!" I exclaimed, unable to hide my sudden burst of excitement. "You were here yesterday. You saw what happened to Ms. Miller." I didn't know for sure that he had, but something had spooked this buck, and I intended to find out what. I held out both hands to show I meant no harm and took one slow step forward.

"No!" he brayed and shook his head, whipping the yellow tape around in a blur. "Leave me alone!"

And just like that he ran off into the forest, the tangled crime scene ribbon twisting in the air behind him.

"Nice one, Sherlock," Octo-Cat quipped, making me feel even worse about scaring off our witness. At least he was calling me Sherlock. Usually he referred to me as Watson, the lovable sidekick rather than the hero.

"Do you think he saw what happened?" I asked, chewing on my lip as I considered the same question.

"I don't know about that, but I do think he's the bad thing I smelled. Yuck." He kicked back his hind legs in the same way he did after using the litter box.

"We need to get him to talk to us," I said.

Octo-Cat shook his head, immediately dismissing my suggestion. "He's prey, Angela. Chasing after him is only going to make him run farther away from you."

"Okay, then what do you suggest?" Seriously, why did I even bother to put forth my own ideas when Octo-Cat was just going to boss me around anyway?

He sighed. "Well, I don't see anything useful in this shed. My guess is the cops cleared it out as part of cleanup. Meanwhile you're not willing to open the door to let us into the house, so I honestly don't know where that leaves us."

"Wait, I have an idea. Follow me." I only turned to make sure he was following me as I turned the corner of the house. Thankfully, he'd fallen right in line, so I led him to the side of the house where I'd spotted the prints leading up to the basement egress window. The prints were no longer visible, but I wondered.

"Hop down there," I ordered, pointing to the window well that sported a patch of gravel before the window. "See if the window is fully latched."

"Oh sure, send the cat. Just because I'm faster, lighter, and smarter. Uh-huh, I see." Octo-Cat complained but he did so with a smile, and when he'd finished saying his piece, he dutifully hopped down to investigate.

"There's no screen," he called back up, then began to paw at the edge of the glass. "It opens out rather than pushing in. I need you to try it."

"No. Can't leave prints," I reminded him.

"Then we're not getting inside. It's as simple as that."

"I'll think of something," I assured him. "Now come back up."

He hopped out to join me, offering a withering glance my way.

"I'm hitting a dead end," I admitted.

He rolled his eyes. "No, you hit a roadblock, and for some reason you refuse to move around it."

Was I being too cautious when it came to leaving my fingerprints behind? I wasn't up to any wrongdoing, and Officer Bouchard knew me well enough to already know about my amateur sleuthing. Plus I was about to be married to the best attorney in town. I probably wouldn't get in much trouble—if any—but still, something about the situation gave me pause.

And as a P.I. it was important I listened to my hunches... And to rely on my partner for help.

"Can you think of anything else we might be missing?" I asked him.

He nodded as if deep in thought. "We only knew her for a couple of weeks, so think back to all of your encounters with her."

"I only met her that first day. Every other time I communicated with her was via animal control or the police or the post office."

"I never met her face-to-face, but I did enjoy peeing on her porch," he said with a self-satisfied smirk.

"Wait." We were close, I could feel it in my bones. "If she didn't see you, how did she know?"

He cocked his head to the side and regarded me suspiciously. "Know what?"

"That you'd peed." That's when I remembered that the animal control officers had come bearing photographs more than once. I ran back toward the porch and began to search the rafters.

"What are you doing?" he asked in a sing-song voice.

I turned to him briefly to explain. "Looking for a hidden camera."

"It's there," he said, motioning with his nose.

"What? Where? And how do you know? You didn't even know there was a camera."

He crinkled his nose. "It's got a weird shimmer to it. It just stands out like a sore thumb. Don't you see it?"

I shook my head, then moved to the side and pointed. "Hot or cold?"

He plopped his butt down and wagged his tail wildly in response. "I don't know what game you're playing here, Angela, but I don't like it."

I growled and stamped my foot, growing very frustrated with this. "Am I close or far away?"

Finally he got it and was able to direct me to the

camera. I grabbed it down, forgetting for a moment about my reluctance to leave prints. *Shoot.*

"We'll take this back to the house, but I think she had more of these set up around the property. There were other pictures, taken from other angles." I wished then that animal control had left the pictures with me so that I could use them to help figure out the camera placements, but no.

Octo-Cat grinned deviously. "You need me to go find them, don't you?"

"I do, but first let's get this one home and see what we can find."

12

ack at home, I did a quick web search on the make and model of the trail cam we'd found on Ms. Miller's porch. Once I understood how the thing was intended to work, I began taking it apart in search of evidence. Even though I followed the directions exactly, I couldn't find the memory card that was meant to store the video feed.

"Am I overlooking it?" I asked Octo-Cat in frustration, but he didn't find anything either.

A scrabbling at the window drew my eye across the room. Pringle stood waving with one hand and pointing at the door with the other. As much as I still hadn't forgiven the raccoon for taking Paisley hostage last week, I did want to hear if he had any theories about what happened next door. His mind was always running at a million miles per minute. Usually that was to my detriment, but occasionally his penchant for overthinking could prove beneficial.

I set the camera down on the table, then moved toward the front door and carefully let myself out onto the porch, blocking the way so Pringle couldn't squeeze past me into the house.

Octo-Cat followed through the pet flap. Even though he wasn't a fan of Pringle, he was a fan of drama. He'd also become invested in this case.

"You got some new tech?" the raccoon said as soon as were standing on the porch with him, all the while rubbing his hands together as if he were washing them in a stream. "I wanna see."

That was right. Our resident raccoon was obsessed with all forms of technology. Gossip too. Which made him the perfect spy whenever he managed to focus on the task at hand. It also meant he had a lot in common with the deceased. He might actually understand what had made Angela Miller tick, because I certainly didn't get it.

Dang it, I needed his help.

"I've got a job for you," I said, praying I wouldn't later come to regret this.

"It'll cost you." Pringle rubbed his hands together faster and faster, an addict on the verge of getting a fix.

I'd given into his insane demands many times before, but now that I knew Pringle a bit better, I knew I could get by with much less. "I will let you play with my cool new tech, if you do me a favor first."

"Favor, favor, yes!" he cried, his eyes growing wide as if he could already see a future in which he had taken possession of his prize.

There were three things I needed his help with, but if I told him the full list at once, he'd get distracted and forget to do any of it. If I told him in the wrong order, he could abscond with the evidence before actually handing it over to me. It was like a strange logic puzzle with only one right answer.

I thought it over for a few minutes to make sure I was happy with my plan of action before revealing said plan to the hyperactive raccoon. I also needed to give him enough details to explain the task without providing too much and making him bored.

"There's a big buck out in the woods," I began, speaking slowly and making sure to enunciate each word. "He wandered into the neighbor's backyard last night and got crime scene tape stuck in his antlers. We need him to talk to us, but both times I've tried, he's gotten frightened and run off. Can you get him to talk?"

"You need a confession? Roger that." He nodded vigorously. "I can torture him with—"

"No!" I screamed so loud, the house behind me seemed to shake. "He's a potential witness, not a suspect, which means NO interrogation, okay? I just need to know what he saw. It may be the clue to cracking this case wide open."

He paused, suddenly becoming stock still as he raised his eyes to meet mine. "What's in it for me?"

"I'll let you check out the new tech, and when we're done using it as evidence, I'll even let you keep it."

He took a step back, considering my offer. "What is it? What does this new tech do?"

"That's part of the fun." I made my eyes wide and my smile wider. "It's a mystery surprise. So are you on board?"

Pringle raised his hand to his chin and rubbed it as he thought, then jumped straight up into the air and shouted, "I'll do it," before turning tail and running off in pursuit of our witness. I just hoped he took it easy on the poor buck who was already scared half out of his mind.

Octo-Cat pawed at my leg to get my attention. "Why didn't you ask him to go into the house and find the missing memory thingy?"

I shuddered. "I'd rather leave my prints all over that place than unleash that little bandit on a big empty house full of potential treasures."

"Good point. So are we breaking in?" A smile stretched between his whiskers, and I could tell he looked forward to a little recreational B and E.

"I already told you—"

He hissed when he realized I still wasn't playing into his paw. "Just put on a pair of gloves, Angela. Seriously, it's not even that hard. We also have more cameras to find. Get with the program."

"I'm having a hard time moving past that deer. It keeps coming back to the yard even though it's clearly frightened. Why do you suppose that is?"

Octo-Cat let out a low, long groan. "I told you. The guy's prey. They aren't the sharpest tools in the shed, if you know what I'm saying."

"In the shed. That's it!" At last he'd given me a lead I could pursue without worry of looking guilty later.

He tilted his head, regarding me with large golden eyes. "What's it?"

"Ms. Miller died in her back shed. She was knocked out by an extra-large bag of deer feed," I reminded him.

"And?"

"She'd only been in town for a couple of weeks, yet somehow she'd definitely managed to make good friends with that buck. She also complained more than once about Paisley scaring off the deer from her yard." I watched Octo-Cat's face the whole time I explained, but rather than appearing enlightened, he looked downright confused.

"So? So what has that got to do with any of this?" he asked with another savage flick of his tail. "Do you think the deer killed her for being late giving him his dinner?"

Okay, now I was irritated too. "Be reasonable," I whined, unable to help myself. "I already said the buck wasn't a suspect. But her apparent obsession with the local deer is the best lead we've got."

My cat rolled his eyes yet again. We may have hit a new record for how many times he could dismiss me that way in a single day. "I thought the best lead we had was the treasure trove of evidence already waiting literally right next door."

I thought about this for a second. Logically, his point was sound, but something inside me was begging me to follow this new hunch.

"Let's split up," I decided at last. "I'll pursue the deer thing, and you work on finding the other cameras and locating the missing memory card."

"Great, but you still have to let me inside." He yawned. If I didn't act fast, I'd lose him to yet another afternoon spent napping in the sun.

"I'll go grab my gloves…"

13

Nan returned from her flash mob right as I was about to climb into my clunky old sedan and pay a visit to the pet store. "Where are you headed in such a hurry?" she asked, coming out of the garage with Paisley trotting happily at her heels.

"I'm investigating a case," I explained, unable to hide the smile that crept across my face. I really did feel most like myself when I was in the thick of a mystery.

Nan narrowed her gaze and stared at me pointedly. "You're snooping after the neighbor, you mean."

I gasped in alarm. Nan had always approved of

my investigative ways. Had she somehow suddenly changed her tune?

My fears were quickly abated, however, when she looked me up and down with a huge smile and said, "And I approve wholeheartedly. Take Paisley with you for a second set of eyes and ears."

At hearing her name, the little dog began to bark excitedly and run quick zooming circles around Nan.

"What will you do here all by yourself?" I asked, giggling at Paisley's playful antics.

"I'm working on a surprise for Grant, and I don't trust you not to go blabbing." She shook her finger at me then laughed good-naturedly. "Actually I'm surprised I've managed to keep it secret for this long. We'll catch each other up when you're back, okay?"

I smiled and nodded before plopping down into my car. "C'mon, Paisley. Let's go to the store!" I called, then lifted the little dog into the car with me when she showed up outside my door. Even though my sedan was close to the ground, Paisley was too frightened to jump into it by herself—a point which Octo-Cat teased her about whenever he got even the slightest chance.

"What store are we going to, Mommy?" Paisley

asked once I had her settled on my lap and the car headed down the long driveway.

"I'm not sure. I'm thinking maybe the pet store to start and then we'll just go from there. I'm hoping to get some info about the local deer, just in case her connection to them somehow got our neighbor killed," I explained, turning onto the main road and letting the steering wheel maneuver back to center beneath my fingers.

Paisley braced herself for the turn, then popped back up on four feet and wagged her tail until it was a blur. "Oh, yes. The deer here are very nice. They wouldn't hurt anyone."

I slowed the car and looked down at the pup on my lap. "Do you know the deer, Paisley?"

"Sometimes they talk to me even though I'm a predator. They don't think I'm very scary since I'm so small." Typically, Paisley would do anything to prove she was a big dog, but now she seemed almost proud that her tiny stature had afforded her some new friends.

Funny how Angela Miller had complained more than once about Paisley scaring off the deer when the Chihuahua was in fact friendly with the local herd. And shame on me for not thinking to ask Paisley about them earlier.

"Do you know a big buck who lives around here?" I slowed the car to nearly a crawl, wanting to stay on the quiet backroads while I was so immersed in our conversation.

"Sure I do," Paisley nodded and yipped. "That's Irving. We used to talk a lot, but lately he's been too scared to say hello." Yes, we were definitely talking about the same deer I'd seen earlier.

Now I stopped the car completely. I could save myself the errand if Paisley already had all the information I needed. "Scared? Why? What did he see?" I asked, pulling the car over to the shoulder.

Paisley hopped up and put her front paws on the car door, peering outside with open joy. "I don't know. He's not talking to me, remember?"

"Right." Well, it was worth a shot. I rolled down the window for my doggie friend and got back to driving.

We drove to a new pet store that had opened up across town, preferring to avoid the scene of a grisly murder that we'd helped solve a couple years prior. This town was filled with too many memories of past cases, and we had a fresh mystery to focus on now.

My phone buzzed from its spot in the cupholder, then it buzzed again. I resisted the urge to check the new messages until Paisley and I pulled into the pet store parking lot and parked.

"What is it, Mommy?" Paisley asked, her paws back on the side door and her tail wagging furiously. She loved car rides, but even more than that she loved visiting new places—or really any place we were willing to let her tag along.

The missed texts were from Charles. Rather than opening them up, I called instead. If he had time to text, then perhaps he also had time for a chat.

"There you are," he said by way of greeting. I could hear the grin underlying his words.

"Here I am," I answered with a lovesick smile as I sighed and laid my head back against the seat rest.

"So," Charles prompted with a soft, breathy laugh. "Tell me about it."

"About what?" I let out a soft chuckle, as if that would somehow prove my innocence.

"I know you went to investigate, and I know you left my text unread on purpose." His words were firm but not angry. He sounded more bemused than anything else. Still, I'd been found out despite my best attempts to be slick.

Oops. "Yeah, sorry about that."

"Hey, your intellectual curiosity and steadfast

commitment to justice are both part of what I love about you. Just be careful, okay? And tell me if I can help."

"I love you too," I said, brimming with joy at the thought this man would be my husband in just a few short weeks. "And what was that you just said about me? Can I use it on my business website to attract some new clients?"

"What's mine is yours, including my words. Have them."

I chuckled and made a mental note to update my site once I'd wrapped the investigation. I then took time to explain the scene last night in greater detail than I'd given him earlier. I also told him about our investigation so far that day and my hunch that somehow the deer were important.

"I don't know, Angie," my fiancé said after a long pause. "She fell and hit her head? That sounds like an accident to me. The police may be right on this one."

"Something just seems off about it all. I can't shake the feeling, you know?" I sighed. I'd really been hoping he would pick up on some small detail I'd missed, that by simply confiding in Charles I'd crack the case wide open.

"I do know. I just don't have any suggestions on

where to look next." His response was earnest, but he also seemed a little disappointed in his inability to assist with this one. "Think of all the clues you've found. The camera didn't have film. The bootprints matched the ones Officer Bouchard was wearing, and the flashlights at night were only seen by your cat. We know he's not the most reliable. What if he made it up to have some fun at your expense?"

"He wouldn't do that," I said, even though we both knew he would—and had many times before. Was I embarking on a wild goose chase here? And was the gut feeling I had more of a guilty conscience than a detective's hunch?

Charles seemed to think so. "Well, then maybe he got confused about what he saw? Maybe it was all a bad dream?"

I picked at the skin on my elbow. Even though everyone else seemed quick to brush this case aside, I still knew something wasn't right next door. Something had happened, and I wouldn't rest until I found out whether or not that something was murder.

14

I clipped Paisley onto the leash I kept in my car, then the two of us headed inside. This pet shop was much smaller than the bigger chain store a couple cities over. The only adoptable pets it sported were various types of freshwater fish, seeing as the retail shop mainly seemed to focus on pet supplies and not pets themselves.

The storefront was narrow with three long aisles that stretched toward the back. An empty counter stood in front of a large tropical fish tank, an old-fashioned cash register stationed on top.

Paisley tugged hard at the lead, and I followed her down the center aisle, right to a display of dog treats. "Can I have one, Mommy? Can I?" she begged, standing on her hind legs and waving her front paws at me repeatedly.

"Yes, once we find what we came here for," I promised, hoping she would at least choose something size-appropriate this time. While it was adorable watching the little dog gnaw on a bone twice her size, I ultimately had to throw away her last chew when it started to stink up the house.

"Can I help you?" A man I hadn't seen before popped his head out from the far aisle and beamed over at me. For a moment I worried he'd overheard me talking with my dog, but then I remembered I was in the company of another pet person. Pet people never questioned someone talking to their animals, and I also hadn't said anything that made it too obvious that Paisley was talking back. My secret was still safe, at least when it came to this particular stranger.

"Hi," I answered with a friendly wave. "I'm Angie. I noticed your shop was new in town and thought I'd come in to check it out and say hello." The store had popped up several weeks ago and I was pretty sure Nan had been in, but I hadn't yet made it by. Judging by the lack of any other customers, things weren't going too well. I'd need to make more of an effort to support local businesses—being as I was a small business owner myself.

"Hello," the man replied with an overenthusiastic wave back. "I'm Frank, and before you can ask, yes, Beans is most definitely around here somewhere."

"Beans?" I asked in a higher pitch than I liked.

"Yes, that's why the store is called Frank and Beans. My mother said it would only confuse people, but I think it's cute. Don't you?"

"Yes. Oh, yes, definitely. Drew me right in." Truthfully, I hadn't even noticed the name of the shop before entering. Some shrewd detective I was.

Frank joined me in the dog supply aisle, and I got a good look at him for the first time. He wore a graphic T-shirt over a long sleeve collared shirt with checks. He also had on khakis that were just a little too long, judging by the bottoms that were torn up and covered in dirt. I didn't recognize the anime on his T-shirt, so I couldn't say for sure, but the busty character with pouted lips and a flirtatious wink hardly seemed appropriate work attire. I shuddered for the single women of Blueberry Bay.

"Is Beans your dog?" I asked conversationally, unable to tear my eyes away from the cartoon cleavage splashed across his chest.

"Nope, Beans is a cat!" Frank caught me looking and blushed, then placed both hands on top of his shirt to hide the graphic. "His full name is Toby Toe Beans McGillicutty. He's a little shy, but I can go get him if you want to say hello."

"Actually I'm a bit short on time, but I was hoping I could ask you a quick question before I go. I will definitely be back to meet Toe Beans though, I promise." It seemed the friendly thing to offer. Whether or not I liked his T-shirt, Frank still seemed like a nice enough guy. There was absolutely no reason to be rude, especially since I had my diamond engagement ring to show off my status as a taken woman.

"Just Beans," Frank corrected, drawing my attention back to his face.

"Right." I nodded once, twice.

He dropped his hands from his chest and used them to make big sweeping gestures as he spoke. "Okay, yeah. So what's your question? I'm happy to help however I can. Mom says it won't be easy competing with the big national chain, but I say that nothing worth doing is ever easy."

"Yes, totally agree with you there." I reached down and grabbed a bag of treats for Paisley, and she immediately began whimpering in anticipation.

"I'm getting this. And I was also hoping to pick up some deer feed. I live by the forest and have quite a few wander through my yard day to day, so I thought it would be nice to make friends."

"Ah, yes, deer are such remarkable creatures." He waved his arms around wildly and knocked a small bag of treats from the shelf. "I'd love to help. And if you come back closer to Christmas I'll be able to. Haven't got any feed in stock now, what with the regulations and all."

I raised an eyebrow as Frank bent down to scoop up the fallen merchandise. "Regulations?"

"It's hunting season, which means feeding the deer is not allowed until the season is over. Otherwise we'd have a whole gaggle of gunners baiting the poor things and then blasting their heads off." He made finger guns and pointed them at me, then frowned and shoved his hands into his pockets.

"Not a fan of hunting, I take it?" I ventured.

"No sirree. Or rather, no ma'am. I'm a proud vegetarian. Although I do make an exception for Beans. It's not healthy to force a carnivore out of its natural diet. He's a pescatarian."

That poor cat. Octo-Cat did enjoy his shrimp, tuna, and lobster rolls, but he'd have my head if I tried to restrict his diet in any way. The one time I bought him reduced calorie food, he made it a point to puke at the foot of my bed every single day until I switched him back to the full-fat stuff.

"Do you know where I might be able to pick up some feed?" I prompted, attempting to steer our conversation back to where I needed it to go.

"Oh, perhaps I didn't explain myself very well. Mother says I'm always talking too fast and going off the rails, which is a pretty weird expression, right? What have conversations got to do with trains? Anyway, I can't sell you any deer feed right now. No one can, as buying and selling the feed is currently illegal." Frank sniffed and ran a hand through his longish hair. I couldn't tell if he was actively growing it out or if he'd just missed one too many haircuts.

I had to think for a minute to decide how much of my case I was willing to share with this new acquaintance. Despite being a touch odd, he was definitely friendly, but he was also incredibly talkative. I couldn't risk him sharing private details with just anyone who walked into his shop. I had to play this cool.

I laughed it off. "Oh, weird. I had no idea. My neighbor asked me to pick some more feed up for her but didn't mention the regulations. She had a burlap sack filled to the brim with I don't know what. Some kind of grain maybe."

He narrowed his eyes at me, suddenly suspicious of me and all my questions. "She must have gotten it before the season started."

"Maybe she did. Do you know where she might have gotten it? Are there any other shops in town that would sell deer feed during the off-season?"

"The big chain place doesn't have it, let me tell you. Their stores are crowded with a hundred types of dog food, but don't even have this one essential. As far as I know, there aren't any others offering it. You'll have to rely on Frank and Beans for all your deer feed needs. In fact, I already have a nice stock waiting in the warehouse seeing as my supplier accidentally sent the shipment months ahead of time. Silly mistake, but at least he's provided free storage space so we don't have to send the full lot back. Anyway, that will be ready to put out the second those regulations are lifted, but for now can I interest you in some wild bird seed?" He began to head for the next aisle, and I dutifully followed along.

"You can feed the birds all year round. You just have to be careful that it's not stolen by squirrels," Frank explained as he motioned toward his supply.

"Although I do have some squirrel feeders too, if that's up your alley."

"Thank you. You've been very helpful." I selected a small bag of bird seed, then put it back. "I'll just take a little time to browse around. I'll let you know when I'm ready to check out."

He nodded enthusiastically. "Oh, yeah, sure. I'll let you browse in peace. I've got some new inventory to sort through anyway. Just holler when you're ready."

When Frank at last disappeared through the swinging doors that separated the front of the store from the back, I scooped Paisley into my arms and whispered, "Now let's go pick the treats you really want."

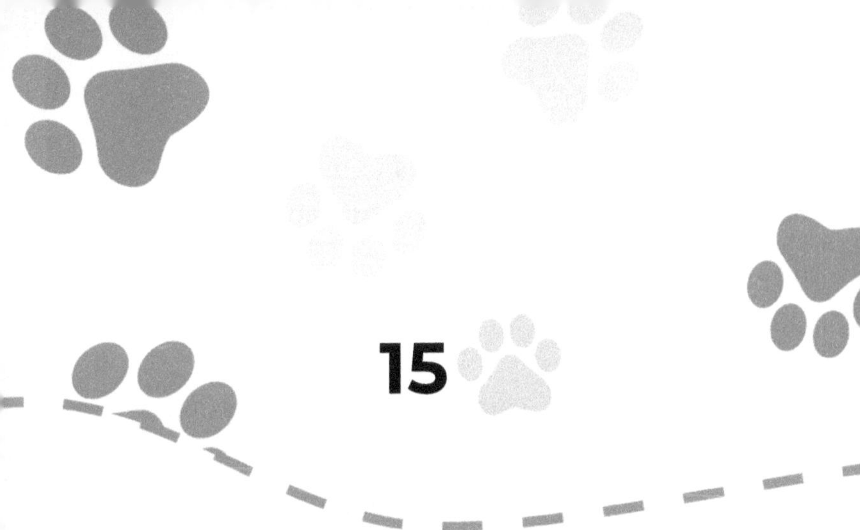

15

"Psssst," a strange voice called from the next aisle over. I ducked my head and went to check it out but found no one.

"I smell a cat," Paisley chimed in just as a little paw reached out from behind some boxes of treats to tap me on the arm.

"Psssst," the voice urged again. "I heard you talking to that dog earlier. I know you can understand me." A pair of green eyes glowed at me from the back of the shelf, but the rest of his small body was ensconced in shadows.

"Beans?" I asked, craning in an effort to get a better look.

"Shhh!" The cat moved forward on the shelf, revealing a long, lanky body covered in orange and white stripes. "Not too loud or my human will come back and ruin everything. Just listen, all right? Nod to show you understand?"

I zipped my lips, nodded, and waited for Beans to say more.

He kept his voice low, which made the whole encounter even more eerie. "I heard you were looking to buy some off-season feed, and let's just say I can hook you up."

I nodded again and offered a spirited thumbs up.

"Great, great. I'll give you the info you need, if you give me what I need." This was feeling more and more like a black market transaction. Who'd have thought that the neighbor's penchant for feeding the local wildlife would lead me down this strange rabbit hole?

"What do you need?" I asked, eager to follow the lead, no matter how strange the trail.

Beans growled and reared back on the shelf. "Shhhh, no talking, remember?!"

I sighed but nodded all the same. As annoying as Octo-Cat could be, Toby Toe Beans McGillicutty was proving to be far worse.

"I overheard Frank tell you about my little problem. You know, the whole fish-only diet? Man, I am dying for a steak. You stop by later and bring me a nice cut of New York strip, I'll see what I can do about getting you that feed." With that, he turned tail and disappeared back behind the shelved goods.

I wanted to call after him to get a little bit more detail about the suggested arrangement, but Frank returned then carrying a big case of canned cat food.

"Still finding everything okay?" he asked, even though it had only been a few minutes since he'd left me on my own.

"Yes, I think I'm ready for you to ring me up," I said, hoping the treats I already had in hand would satisfy Paisley seeing as Beans had interrupted us before she could pick something out for herself.

Frank sang an old rock tune under his breath as he scanned the two items I'd selected, then offered a closed-lip grin and wished me a good day. "Come back often and buy more," he called after me just as I was headed for the door. "Help me prove mother wrong about the viability of my business choices!"

As soon as we were in the car, I opened the bag of treats and offered one to Paisley, which she happily accepted, wagging tail and all.

"That was pretty weird, huh?" I asked.

"Cats are always pretty weird," she mumbled as

she licked at my hand. "But I still like them anyway!"

I waited for her to finish before putting the car in drive and heading to the grocery store. I hoped Beans would be willing to accept a raw steak, because I didn't have time to waste preparing it, especially when any seasoning choices I made could upset the feline and cause him to demand fresh payment. I may not know Beans well, but I knew cats.

I had to leave Paisley in the car while I ran into the grocery store to secure the bribe. Once purchased, I wrapped the meat in a bundle of napkins I pulled from my glove compartment and jammed it in my purse, then drove straight back to the pet store.

Frank had apparently seen me pull back up and stood waiting at the shop door. He held it open with a giant grin, forcing me to squeeze past him to gain entry. "Welcome back. I knew I'd see you again. I just didn't realize it'd be so soon!"

"Well, I thought more about it and realized I would definitely be needing a larger bag of bird seed, what with all the feathery friends who come to roost in my yard. I didn't want anyone to miss out, so I decided to stock up a bit better before putting anything out."

Frank bobbed his head enthusiastically. "Oh, yes, good idea. I'd recommend the Parks brand. Here, let me show you." He began to stroll down one of the aisles and motioned for me to follow.

"Actually, I'm going to spend some time comparing each brand to its online reviews to make sure I come to an informed decision," I countered, having to think quick to buy some alone time. "I hope you don't mind."

"As long as you're buying something, you can go about it however you please. If you need a real expert's opinion, though, you know where to find me." He turned back toward me and winked before heading to the front of the store. Luckily, the bird seed was in the far back of the store, giving me a small semblance of privacy as I worked on my exchange of meat for information with the ravenous Beans.

I stooped down on the floor, tilted so my back was facing the front of the store, fished my cell phone out of my purse, and raised it to my ear. This position would afford me some secrecy as I unpackaged the steak, and the phone would give me a ready excuse if Frank overheard me talking to the animals.

I clucked my tongue and whispered, "Here, kitty, kitty, kitty."

Paisley wagged her tail and let out a sharp bark.

"No bark," I told her plainly, more or less certain her cry had drawn the store owner's attention.

"Psssst, I'm over here."

I turned my head toward the source of the voice, but Beans yelled at me. "No, don't look. Just listen."

I nodded, wondering if every time I interacted with this cat, he'd demand I shut off another one of my senses.

"You got the goods. I can smell it. Now here's what I need you to do. Unpackage the steak and place it on the floor in front of you. I'll come inspect to make sure everything is good, and then I'll tell you what you need to know."

I nodded and reached into my purse, freeing the offering from its foam and plastic packaging and then wrapping the trash in the bundle of napkins before jamming the wad back in my purse. I set the steak on the floor as instructed and waited.

"Mommy?" Paisley cried with joy. "Is that for me?"

I had to pick her up one-handed so that she wouldn't gobble down our payment before it could be collected.

I glanced to the side even though Beans had warned me not to and saw him creeping forward, slow and close to the ground.

He stopped in front of me to inspect the New York strip and give it a couple licks. "Yes, this will do quite nicely."

I tapped on my phone and said, "Hello. Yes. What did you want to tell me again?"

Beans appraised me for a moment and nodded. "Ah, a clever ruse. Although you don't need to be all that clever to outsmart Frank. Do you think it was his idea to start this store? No. It was all part of my plan to get some variety in my diet so I'm not stuck eating fish food my entire nine lives. Anyway, the warehouse guy is named Steve. He comes here twice per week to deliver stock—in fact, he was just here yesterday, which means he probably won't be back for a few more days. The man you're looking for drives a big white truck with a picture of a crab and a lighthouse on it."

"Yes, I'd be happy to arrange a meeting," I told the imaginary speaker on the other end of my phone. "What days work best for you and Steve?"

"I can't say. He's never consistent. Something doesn't quite smell right about the guy, if you catch my drift. But if he's got Frank's deer feed in the warehouse, I'm sure he'd be happy to sell it to you for a tidy profit."

"Thank you," I said, then stuck my phone in my purse and reached down to pat the orange tabby on his head.

He grabbed the giant hunk of meat and ran off to hide somewhere, and I grabbed the largest bag of bird seed the store had on offer, ready to hightail it out of there and put the next stage of my plan in action.

16

"**O**kay, my friend, what have you got for me?" I asked my web browser as I pulled up Google and input my search terms: *Crab, lighthouse, warehouse, Blueberry Bay, Maine.*

The first few results were for actual lighthouses, fish markets, and local restaurants, but on the second page of the completed search I found a link to Scotch on the Docks Storage Services, owned by one Steven Scotch. That had to be it, although I hadn't the faintest idea how the crab on the logo related to the name of the company. It was definitely a match though.

The business address given online was for a post office box rather than a physical location, and trying to call the number listed resulted in a prere-corded message that informed me the number had been disconnected.

Very strange for someone I knew from a first-hand account was still actively in business. In the absence of any better ideas, I decided to drive down to the docks and see if I got lucky.

As I drove through town to the bay that gave this region its name, I wondered how Octo-Cat was faring in his search of the neighbor's homestead. Had he already found the missing memory card and remaining cameras? Or had he gotten bored and decided to take a nap? Either was just as likely, but I'd find out soon enough, I supposed. My thoughts also drifted to Pringle as I wondered whether the raccoon had managed to get the fright-ened buck witness to speak yet. It was a bit odd that the three of us were pursuing this case from entirely different angles, but it also gave me confi-dence that we'd have it solved in no time. Even if both cat and raccoon had slacked off, I was still making good progress on my own—or rather, with Paisley at my side.

I pulled into a large, mostly empty parking lot, took several deep breaths, and made my way down to the water. I didn't love being back on the wharf, considering my last visit here had led to my near drowning at the hands of a pistol-wielding madwoman. This time, however, I'd come during daylight hours and of my own volition. I also had Paisley to help keep me safe. Sure, the little Chihuahua couldn't do much in a fight, but she had a habit of barking at even the slightest perceived threat. More often than not, she sounded the alarm for minor things like blowing leaves or an approaching mail carrier, but still, it was good knowing she'd be watching my back, my front, and really all sides of me as I investigated the area.

After a short walk through the area, I found a crew actively unloading a large ship on the quay and marched right up to say hello. "Hey, hello! I'm looking for Steve Scotch, Scotch on the Docks Storage. Do you know where I might find him?"

At first it didn't seem as if any of them had heard me. The handful of burly men and women just kept moving goods from the ship to the land. They made a tiny, efficient army of sorts in their matching dark blue coveralls and heavy steel-toed boots. I'm sure I appeared ridiculous to them with my polka-dotted maxi dress, foam flip-flops, and Chihuahua companion, but I made no apologies for my fashion choices. I only felt sorry for bothering them when they clearly had so much work to do.

"Hi, excuse me," I tried again, raising a hand to better attract their attention. "Do any of you know where I can find Steve Scotch?"

This time they definitely heard me. A couple of the men grumbled to one another while staring daggers in my direction and making me decidedly uncomfortable. I was just contemplating how far I should push my luck when one of the female crew members set down her load and jogged over to speak with me. "Careful who you go asking for around here. Steve Scotch is persona non grata after he stiffed us on our last job."

I winced at this revelation. "I'm sorry."

She dragged her forearm across her brow and let out a heavy breath. "Not your fault, but as far as I know the guy's gone out of business. We haven't seen him around here in close to a month."

I nodded. "Okay, thanks for letting me know." No wonder the other workers had seem irked by my presence. I'd come out of nowhere to remind them of a bad memory. For all they knew, I was looking for the prodigal warehouser because the two of us were friendly. Not because I suspected him of murder. They didn't need to know all the details, especially since they didn't know where Steve Scotch had disappeared to. On all fronts, it seemed the man had gone out of business, yet Beans had confirmed that he still visited the pet store twice per week with new deliveries—and he'd even been there as recently as yesterday. What was going on? And how did it relate to Angela Miller's death? I was so close to solving this case I could taste it. I'd just need to go back to the pet store and talk to Frank or Beans or perhaps both.

But what could I say to explain my line of questioning? Beans was a cat. I was lucky he knew as much as he did and that he was willing to share that information with me for a relatively low payoff. Frank, on the other hand, was clearly uncomfortable with the entire idea of buying and selling off-season feed. If I went back and asked more questions about it, I'd need to explain everything...

Or I could get Nan to go in and specifically ask after the warehouse guy. Maybe she could say she needed to store some things and that Steven had been recommended but she'd had a hard time getting in touch, and then mention seeing his van outside the pet supply store the day prior. Yes, that would certainly beat staking out a strip mall. That was far too conspicuous, considering I didn't want to draw attention to myself or this investigation. Sending in Nan as a collaborative agent made the most sense, which meant I needed to head home now, clue Nan in on the plan, and catch up with the others.

I thanked the dock worker again and then turned back in the direction of the parking lot. Just then, however, Paisley started to growl. I glanced down and found her hackles raised and teeth bared.

Panic shot through me in an instant. I held my breath and asked, "What is it, girl?"

Paisley growled again, then ran forward at a feverish pace. I wasn't sure if we were running toward something or running away, but run I did.

Paisley darted right through a flock of seagulls that had gathered on the pier, barking furiously, then circling back around to chase off the stragglers.

When I finally caught up, I scooped her into my arms. "What was that all about? Is everything okay?"

"They were saying mean things about you, Mommy," she whimpered and squirmed in my arms. "One of them was even going to poop on your head!"

One of the seagulls glided back down and

landed on the wooden railing. "I hear you're getting married, Angie Russo," the bird said in an eerily familiar voice. *Alpha!* He was the very same seagull I'd ousted from control of his flock after Charles and Pringle had proven he'd hired a cat to take out a rival flock to expand his territory. Since then we'd become good friends with his successor Bravo and Bravo's adopted daughter Abigull, but I hadn't seen the former head honcho again until now.

"What do you want from me?" I asked, my voice shaky with fright. This guy had murdered dozens of his own kind, and he definitely had an axe to grind with me for revealing his crimes and getting him exiled.

"Oh, you've already done more than enough for me. I just figured it's time I return the favor. See you at the ceremony," he said before flying off.

Paisley barked at him until he was out of sight, and I added another item to my mental to-do list. I'd need to make sure to seagull-proof my outdoor wedding. How hard could that be?

17

By the time I returned home, I was well past exhausted. Still, I had to keep going, especially when I sensed I was so close to finding out what really happened to old Ms. Miller next door.

I'd hardly gotten through the door when Octo-Cat descended upon me, a look of derision etched across his furry face.

"What took you so long?" he demanded, his mouth held partially open to reveal his sharp incisors.

I dropped my purse onto the bench by the door and pushed off my shoes. "First we went to that new pet store in town. Talking to the owner didn't give us any real leads, but then—"

"Can it, Angela. I don't care."

I glanced down to find him glaring at me. Whatever was upsetting him, he clearly blamed me for it. "But you just asked—"

"Again, I do not care." He growled and sauntered away as if I wasn't worth wasting any more time on. "You have already wasted enough of my time. Now follow me."

He led me over to the dining room table where I'd left both my laptop and the camera we'd filched from the neighbor's porch. A third item also sat waiting beside them.

"Is this..?" I asked, unable to hide my surprise.

"Yes, I completed my primary objective in hardly any time at all. Then I was left to wait in agony as you twiddled those opposable thumbs—thumbs I could have made very good use of, by the way. Now turn on the video. I've been so anxious to see what's on this thing that I've hardly been able to eat or nap all day." He sighed heavily and then yawned to further emphasize his point.

I avoided making a sarcastic remark, especially one that involved his weight or activity level. After all, I was genuinely curious what we'd find in this footage too.

I popped the small chip into the SD card slot on

my laptop and waited for it to load. Most of the footage was boring, still shots of Ms. Miller's front porch. Occasionally, she'd come out to water the flowers or to yell into her speaker phone—about me, no doubt. I couldn't say for sure since our feed had no sound. I zoomed through the footage faster and faster, about to give up when...

"There!" Octo-Cat shouted and lifted a paw to motion at the screen. "Stop and go back a little."

I did as instructed, then watched in silent horror as my cat appeared on camera, squatted in the center of the porch, and did his business.

"Haha, nice one," Octo-Cat cheered on his past self with clear pride.

"You're disgusting," I said, shaking my head. "If you're not going to take this seriously, then there's no point in even watching."

I zipped the footage ahead again. We'd now made it to yesterday morning. Later that day, the cranky old neighbor would be found dead. Yet again, I was just about to give up and exit out of the feed when something important caught my eye. There on the screen, I watched as a large man strode up the porch steps and knocked on Ms. Miller's front door. He appeared to be the rough-and-tumble sort with a bald head, thick beard, and worn-down clothing.

Could it be…?

I zoomed in to get a closer look, which only made the image grainier. Frustrated, I paused and looked to my kitty companion. "Octo-Cat, can you tell what he's got on his arm there?"

"Of course, I can tell. Feline vision is far superior to human vision, as is our hearing, our intellect, our beauty, our—"

"I'm going to stop you right there, your greatness," I cut in with a snort. "I just need to know what's on his arm. Little bit of help here?"

Octo-Cat chuckled and shook his head. "What would you do without me, Angela? Seriously? It's right in front of your eyes, clear as day, and still you can't tell that the thing on his arm is a drawing of a crab."

"A drawing? Like a tattoo?"

"How should I know? You're not cool enough to get any ink of your own, so I've never seen one in person before."

Well, I couldn't let him get away with that assertion. I rushed to defend myself. "Correction, I am cool enough for a tattoo. It's that I'm not brave enough. There's a big difference between the two."

He just shrugged and turned away, probably rolling his eyes at me. Whatever.

I started the video again and watched as Angela Miller opened the door and appeared to have a heated exchange with the man. He shifted, affording me a better view of his forearm ink, and that's when it all clicked into place.

I grabbed my phone and reopened the web search I'd done earlier from the pet store parking lot. I zoomed in on the logo I'd found on the woefully out-of-date website and held it up to my laptop screen.

"What do you think?" I asked my partner as I too glanced from one device to the other. "Do these two crabs match?"

"Yes, they're the same," he confirmed without further comment.

"Steve Scotch," I said with an enormous sense of relief at having identified the mystery visitor. "He's definitely our man."

Now my cat looked irritated with me once again. "Great, but who's Steve Scotch?"

"You'd know if you had let me tell you about my day instead of interru—"

"Then tell me already," he insisted, the irony clearly escaping him.

I sighed but did as he asked. Even when I was one hundred percent in the right, it wasn't enough to make the cat back down on his opinions. And we had too much to discuss for me to waste time lecturing him on manners. As far as those things went, my words always went right in one fur-lined ear and out the other. For the moment, though, I had Octo-Cat's rapt attention.

"Angela," he gasped when I'd finished. "Why didn't you tell me any of this earlier? These are key facts for our investigation."

"I tried to, but—"

He held up a paw to silence me once more, then hopped off the table and glanced back up at me. "We have clear evidence that connects this shady warehouse guy with the stiff. It's time to go to the police."

"Right. And how will we explain how we happened upon this evidence, or even why we find it significant? My key informant is a cat named Beans, and we illegally secured that footage. We don't need Charles here to tell us that this won't be admissible in court. We have a connection, but not a motive. Not yet. We need to find those other cameras and see what they reveal." I hated the words even as I spoke them. Now we were operating on far more than a hunch, but it still wasn't enough to prove anything to the authorities.

"I already found the other cameras," he informed me with a pointed look.

My ears perked up, and my heart raced with excitement. "You did? Good kitty. But, uh, where are they?"

"Couldn't get them down without you," he said with a snarl. "But now that you've finally decided to show up for the job, let's go."

I swallowed back my retort so as not to waste any more of our time. Once this case was fully solved, I could give my cat an earful about his attitude and how it could sometimes hurt my feelings.

I didn't expect him to care, but at least I would feel a little better.

18

"I found two other cameras," Octo-Cat informed me as I followed him across the front lawn. "Both are in the forest. One points toward our house, and the other points toward her house. They weren't too hard to spot. I'm sure even you would have found them eventually if you'd just tried."

"Great. Lead the way," I said, even though he already was.

My cat made a beeline through the woods until we came upon a thick tree with two cameras mounted on its trunk.

I positioned myself in front of the first and stared out across the forest, trying to determine the visibility of each camera. Despite the thick copse, I could just make out our front porch if I craned my head at the right angle.

I then moved to the other side when a flash of bright yellow caught my eye. It was coming from the neighbor's backyard. Our witness!

I crept closer, not wanting to startle the buck away before I had a chance to speak with him.

"Um, excuse me! What about the cameras?" Octo-Cat hissed but then fell into step beside me anyway.

The buck didn't notice our approach, not when he was so focused on whatever was in front of him. His massive brown body blocked it from view, but my ears soon revealed what my eyes could not.

"Tell me what you know, or it's venison for you!" Pringle shouted and lifted his arms high above his head to make himself appear more threatening.

Irving shook his head back and forth, the yellow tape still tangled in his sizable rack. "Please. Please. I don't know anything."

Oh no! I never should have trusted the raccoon to do such an important job. This deer was already terrified enough without Pringle threatening to eat him. Besides, I happened to know the masked critter had a strong preference for processed food.

He'd never eat fresh game, not so long as there was a steady supply of trash cans by the curb each week.

"Pringle, get out of here," I commanded through clenched teeth, careful not to raise my voice and make the situation even worse. I softened my voice when speaking with the buck. "Irving, I'm sorry about him. Nobody is going to hurt you."

"H-how did you know m-m-my name?" he stammered.

I smiled to reassure him that I was friendly. "I believe we have a mutual friend in Paisley."

"The little dog? Yes, I like her, but I don't like him." Irving turned to Pringle with wide eyes as if he'd suddenly frozen and was now caught staring into oncoming traffic. "I do not like him at all," he finished, hardly moving his mouth as he spoke.

And that was when Paisley came zooming onto the scene. "Did you call me, Mommy? Oh, hi, Irving."

The buck still stood staring in fright at the raccoon.

"Is this guy bothering you?" Paisley asked with a ruff. Irving didn't say a thing, but his doggie friend still charged at the trash panda, teeth bared, hackles raised. "Get out of here, you no-good meanie!" she cried and yipped and just generally created a huge ruckus.

"I was just trying to help!" Pringle ground out as he scampered off into the trees.

"Wow," Octo-Cat said flatly, his expression bored. "You actually did a dog thing, Paisley. I'm impressed."

She wagged her tail happily and gave her big brother a kiss on the cheek, unaware that he'd actually been insulting her.

"Ick. How many times do I have to tell you? No kissing the cat!" The tabby tensed at her affection, but Paisley was undeterred. She gave him a good lick-down, then trotted off to roll in a fresh pile of deer droppings. Gross. I'd have to hose her off once we got back home.

But first I had a witness to question.

"Irving, I know you're frightened, but I promise none of us will hurt you," I said, finally breaking him of his whole cliche deer-in-headlights thing. "We're just trying to figure out what happened to your friend who lived in this house."

"She died," the buck whispered reverently. "I saw the whole thing. It was terrible."

"Is that why you've been so afraid lately?" I ventured gently.

He shook his head, waving the tattered crime scene tape around some more.

I approached slowly. "Do you mind if I untangle this for you while we talk?" I asked, raising a tentative hand toward his rack.

"Please, it's been bothering me so much, but nothing I've done has gotten it unstuck."

I lifted both hands and got to work while Irving continued to open up.

"And to answer your question, I'm afraid because it's hunting season. Each year I manage to evade the hunters, and each year I'm an even bigger prize for them as my antlers grow. They all want to turn me into a trophy... or dinner. It's a horrible, barbaric thing." He shuddered and froze again.

I made soft shushing noises and gently patted his flank. "I'm sorry. It must be very hard to live like that, in constant fear that someone is after you."

I waited for him to thaw again before resuming my work on the mess in his antlers.

"I like these woods because there aren't any large predators around," he revealed. "You know, other than humans. I decided to make it my home when I met Angela. She gives me my dinner each

night and talks nicely to me. At least she did until
—" Irving choked on a sob.

"Until?" I prompted as I continued to work on
the mess in his antlers.

"It's all my fault," he bleated. "She was getting
me my dinner, same as every night, when her grip
slipped. My dinner crushed her to death, and there
was so much blood. I tried to help her, but I got
afraid and ran away. When I came back, the police
were here."

"And you got stuck in the crime scene tape," I
finished for him. It all made perfect logical sense,
but it still didn't explain all the evidence we'd
found.

"I've been running ever since. I keep checking
back to see if Angela will return, but I'm afraid
she's really dead. I'm going to miss her," he snuffled
and wailed, inadvertently jerking his antlers out of
my reach. "She was the nicest human I ever met."

My heart went out to Irving. Ms. Miller too. It
just went to show that people are incredibly
complex and confusing creatures. The same lady
was an enemy to me but a friend to Irving.
Somehow she was both of those things at the same
time, even though it seemed that shouldn't have
been possible.

"You said she lost her grip? That it was an accident?"

Irving nodded. "Yes, I'm positive. Oh, it was so terrible. I just hate thinking about it."

"I promise not to bother you much longer." I finally freed him of the torn yellow ribbon. Now I just had one last question to ask. "Are you sure you didn't see anyone else around? Anyone who may have hurt Angela?" I knew I was leading the witness, but we weren't exactly in court here. If Ms. Miller's death had really been an accident, then what was with the dodgy warehouse guy paying her a visit?

Irving raked his antlers against a nearby tree and let out a giant sigh of delight. He seemed to smile as he turned to me, but then his mouth fell open in fear as he revealed, "I did see someone, but not until after she was gone. He came last night with a bright light..."

19

After we finished talking with Irving, Octo-Cat, Paisley, and I returned to the woods. I couldn't dislodge the trail cams from the thick tree trunk, but I was able to open them up and snag the memory cards.

My two furry sidekicks wanted to watch the feed of our house so they could admire themselves on camera, but I put them off in favor of watching Ms. Miller's yard instead.

Sure enough, Irving appeared at the same time each evening to collect his dinner, and the old woman spent a fair amount of time standing with him and speaking words I couldn't hear. The camera didn't afford a view into the shed, but the panicked deer moving back and forth as he investigated the scene confirmed when the death had happened—and that no one else had been around.

"So it wasn't a murder, after all," I concluded with a sigh. I probably should have been happy, but the end result was the same. A woman was dead.

"Well, there you go," Octo-Cat said with an unhappy sneer. "Case closed. I can't believe you had me high-footing it all over the place for absolutely nothing. I deserve a raise."

"But we had to know for sure," I reminded him. This had happened practically in our own backyard. How could we not investigate?

Octo-Cat remained unconvinced. "Why? Nobody was paying us. We didn't even like the lady. You tricked me into all of this by pointing out how superior I am to you. Lesson learned. Just because you need me doesn't mean I need you."

I put a hand to my heart. "Ouch, Octo-Cat. That really hurts me. I thought we were friends. Besides, if you don't need me, then who is going to open your cans of food? Who is going to take care of you to your exact specifications? Who is—?"

"Mommy!" Paisley barked, and I turned to her with a quizzical glance. "I'm sorry to interrupt, but look!"

I followed her gaze back to the screen. The feed

showed night-time now, but the rear floodlights had been illuminated by motion.

"Just wait," Paisley instructed, her eyes wide and glistening. "He came before, and I'm pretty sure he's coming back again."

Sure enough, a large man stalked across the yard and disappeared into the shed. When he reemerged he was carrying several small burlap bags stacked on top of one another. I couldn't make out his tattoo of a crab, but still I knew we had our guy.

"That's why the shed had been cleaned out," I remembered. "We thought it was the police, but no. Steve Scotch came back to take the deer feed. But why would he steal deer feed? Was it just so he could sell it again?"

Octo-Cat scoffed. "That hardly seems like a profitable venture."

"Something weird is definitely going on here. We know now that it wasn't murder, but think about this for a second." I really felt like I had all the pieces of the puzzle and just needed to see how they fit together. I racked my brain for everything I'd learned about Steve Scotch and the deer feed to put all the clues on display for my companions.

"Go on. I'm listening," Octo-Cat droned impatiently.

Paisley stayed quiet but wagged her tail, which was all the confirmation I needed to continue.

"Okay, here goes," I said, holding up my hands so I could tick off each detail on my fingers. "Angela Miller was feeding the deer next door. But right now there aren't any local shops that will sell deer feed since it's illegal to do so during hunting season."

"She could have brought the feed with her when she moved," my cat argued with a flick of his tail. He liked to be the one to put all the clues together, but this time I had him beat.

I shook my head. "She could have, but I don't think that's what happened."

"Okay, genius," he hissed. "What have you got?"

"She went to the pet store hoping to make a purchase, but Frank probably gave her the same lecture he gave me. Knowing how she was with us, she probably gave him an earful, creating quite the scene."

He nodded. "Right. I'm with you so far."

"Okay, here's where we have to join our two threads. The cat Beans mentioned that the warehouse guy had been at the store yesterday. That's the same day Angela died. My guess is he overheard her yelling at Frank and then approached her once she'd left the store offering to sell her some feed at a significant markup."

"But you said she hadn't brought feed with her when she moved." Octo-Cat grinned at having caught me up, but he hadn't. Not really.

"I think maybe she brought some but ran out quickly when a huge buck started showing up for dinner every night. She needed to replenish her supply or risk losing her friend."

"Oh, that's sad!" Paisley chimed in, her ears drooping. Honestly, I hadn't even been sure she was listening since she still had her eyes glued to the footage on my laptop.

"It is sad, but more than that it's unlucky. When I was talking with Frank, he mentioned that his supplier had accidentally sent the feed several months early but was paying for it to be warehoused because of the mistake. Frank promised he'd have some for me to buy the second it became okay to sell again. Here comes a third thread."

I paused, but neither animal had anything to say.

"Once I figured out the name of the storage company, I looked it up online. The address was a

P.O. box and the number had been disconnected. I went down to the docks to ask after Steve Scotch, but one of the workers told me that he'd pretty much disappeared a month back after refusing to pay them for a job. All signs point to him being out of business..."

"Except he's still going to the pet store twice per week and he came by our neighbor's house at least one time," Octo-Cat pointed out.

"Exactly."

Octo-Cat yawned. "So where does that leave us?"

"I think Steve Scotch quit his job because he found a better offer. But he still needed a front so he kept up the whole Scotch on the Docks facade."

"A front for what?" He yawned again. If I didn't hurry, I'd lose him entirely.

"That's what I'm trying to figure out. Whatever it is, it involves the pet store though."

"Do you think Frank is a bad guy?" Paisley whined. "He seemed very nice to me."

"Maybe, but it's also possible he simply doesn't know what's going on. If he were to blame, then I doubt he'd have been so forthcoming with the details. Also wouldn't he have tried to sell me the feed under the table when I came in asking about it?"

"What's under the table?" Paisley wanted to know, squirming to get a better view.

"It's just an expression for when people do things the wrong way," I explained with a laugh.

Her tail drooped in disappointment, softening my heart.

"I have an idea. Let's all go to the pet store. Do you wanna go on another car ride?" I asked in a hyper babyish voice that always got Paisley riled up.

"Hard pass," Octo-Cat said, hopping down from the table and sauntering away. "I need a nap. But let me know how it goes. Also don't forget about my raise."

20

When I arrived at Frank and Beans a short while later, I found a police cruiser already sitting in the parking lot outside.

Inside, I found Officer Bouchard standing on one side of the counter and Frank standing on the other. I let myself in, but neither seemed to notice my arrival.

"I already told you, officer. I would never sell deer feed off season. My professional ethics are a point of pride." He spotted me standing in the doorway and offered a broad smile. "Oh, hello again. Three times in one day. I'm starting to think you're addicted to my store."

"What's going on here?" I asked, picking up

Paisley to cradle her to my chest and to give her a better view of the scene.

Officer Bouchard frowned. "That's not really—"

"They're accusing me of selling stolen goods," Frank interrupted, all too happy to share. "Can you believe that? Me? I can assure you I follow the letter of the law."

And there it was, that final piece that brought the whole picture together. I turned to Officer Bouchard, unable to hide my excitement. "The big bag that crushed Angela Miller, there was something other than deer feed inside, wasn't there?"

"But how could you possibly—Angie, you've been investigating again, haven't you?" He put both hands on his hips and glared at me.

I shrugged and offered a small smile.

The policeman sighed. "Fine. Just tell us what you know, but don't say a thing about how you know it. I really don't want to have to take you in for questioning."

I nodded and shared all that I had learned.

"So you're saying this Steven Scotch guy used the pet store as a front for his black market activities?" Officer Bouchard summarized when I was halfway through.

"Yes, he quit showing up at the docks about a

month ago, around the same time Frank first set up for business. He still comes by this place twice per week, even though all signs point to him having gone out of business."

Bouchard gave Frank a pointed look. "Care to amend your story at all?"

"No," I cut in at once. "Frank's not guilty. Steve was using his products to hide the fenced goods, which is why he's in and out of the pet shop so much despite it not being too busy yet. My guess is Steve overheard Angela Miller when she came in searching for deer feed. When Frank wouldn't sell it to her, he saw the opportunity to make some quick cash and offered to hook her up for a price. But then he must have given her the wrong bags. That's why he came back to her house, asking to get the feed back."

"How do you...?" He shook his head and frowned again. "No, no, don't tell me. Just keep going."

"Then he came back later that night, found the shed unlocked, and took all the remaining feed bags," I concluded, almost feeling like I should throw up jazz hands at the big reveal. Thankfully, I managed to restrain myself

The policeman nodded thoughtfully. "Thank

you for telling me just enough to put me on the right path. Looks like I need to bring Steve Scotch in for questioning. Have a good day," he said to Frank, then turned toward me with a raised brow. "Stay out of trouble, you hear?"

Frank and I stood in silence for a few moments after Bouchard left. Finally he shook his head, laughed, and said, "Okay, so what can I sell you this time?"

"Actually," I confessed, feeling a bit sheepish, "I was only here to investigate. The lady who died lived next door to me." I pulled a card from my purse and handed it to him.

"Angie Russo, Pet Whisperer P.I." he read in apparent awe. "You can talk to animals?

I forced a laugh. "Of course not, don't be silly. It's just a gimmick, and an excuse for bringing my cat and dog with me on all my cases." I still hated that Nan and my mother had saddled me with a name that skirted so close to revealing my secret.

Frank's eyes grew wide. "You have a cat? We should set up a playdate with Beans."

"Yeah, sure." I knew Octo-Cat would hate being forced to spend time with another cat, especially one as weird as Beans, but I'd leave the idea in my back pocket in case I ever needed a creative way to punish him.

"I have to get home," I told Frank, who still stood there studying my card. "But I promise I'll be back to do some real shopping."

I wasn't sure he'd heard me since he kept studying my card as if it held the secrets to life, the universe, and everything. When my farewell went unmet, I quietly let myself outside and then drove home to share the news with Nan and Octo-Cat.

* * *

"So it wasn't a homicide," Nan summarized as she sipped at her tea. We were sitting together in the living room now as I went over the encounter I'd had with Officer Bouchard and Frank at the pet store. Octo-Cat was still off napping somewhere, which meant I'd have to recount everything again later, but I didn't mind.

I shook my head. "Nope, but her death revealed another crime."

"Funny that." Nan wrapped both hands around her mug and sighed. "This is why I keep up with my meditation, you know?"

I scrunched my brow in confusion. I was often

confused when it came to Nan, but that was part of her charm. She gave me a knowing look. "That Angela died because of some silly accident. She slipped, hit her head, and then she was gone. That's some majorly bad karma."

"It was just dumb luck."

"Not luck. Karma. It's one of the strongest forces in the universe, and let me assure you, it is anything but dumb. That woman put lots of bad energy out, and all of a sudden it came zipping back at her." Nan took another sip of tea.

I didn't know what to say to that, so I simply shrugged. A gentle knock at the window behind me drew my attention and provided a nice change of topic.

Pringle sat on the ledge holding a bouquet of flowers. When he saw he had my attention, he held them up in offering, then motioned to the door.

"Be right back," I told Nan, who seemed content to sit with her tea and her thoughts as I crept onto the porch to speak with the raccoon.

"These are for you," Pringle said, holding the flowers out to me once more.

"Thank you. They're beautiful."

"I got them from the neighbor's porch. She won't be needing them anymore."

It took great effort to hold back my groan. I tried to focus on the fact that Pringle had brought me a peace offering instead of the fact that he'd filched said offering from the neighbor.

"I'm sorry," he said, hardly above a whisper.

"No, that's not right," he muttered to himself, then got down on one knee and declared with a great sweeping gesture, "I'm sorry!"

I shifted my weight from foot to foot, unable to believe what I was hearing. "You're sorry? For what?"

"For all the times I have hurt you or others because of my actions. I thought long and hard after what happened with that deer."

"And with Paisley," I added with a glower.

"And with Paisley," he confirmed. "I didn't mean to cause any trouble, honest. I just like being included, but sometimes I go about it the wrong way."

I offered him a kindly smile. "That's very big of you, Pringle. I appreciate the apology."

"I'm starting a twelve-step program," he said with a grin. "The seagulls told me about it. When I'm finished, I won't have a drinking problem anymore."

I bit back a laugh. "But Pringle, you don't have a drinking problem."

"Oh, right! The program usually helps people who drink too much alcohol, but the seagull suggested I could do the same twelve steps to help with my behavioral issues. There's a nice group of people who meet every night at a church not far from here. I already scoped it out. There's a perfect spot where I can sit at the window and look in."

"Well, that sounds lovely. Good on you, Pringle."

"Yeah, you know that Alpha isn't such a bad guy, after all."

"Wait, you said the seagulls told you about the program."

"Yeah, well, really just one seagull. Alpha. Remember him?"

Fear enveloped my heart. This was the same bird who'd threatened me earlier that day. Was he using Pringle to get to me? How could getting the raccoon help he so clearly needed ultimately serve to hurt me? What was this bird's big plan?

"Thank you again, Pringle." I raised the flowers to my nose and took a big whiff to show my appreciation. "I'm proud of you."

"Yay, I'm doing it!" he cheered before scampering off the porch and around the house.

I headed inside to put my ill-gotten bouquet in some water. I'd only just closed out one case and already I had another.

What on earth was that devious seagull up to now?

Wedding bells are ringing for Angie and Charles, and everyone's come back to Blueberry Bay to celebrate... What could possibly go wrong?

Get your copy of *Scheming Sphynx*, so that you can keep reading this series today!

* * *

Pssst... If you absolutely loved this book and want even more, make sure you **sign up for Molly's newsletter**. When you do, you'll receive an exclusive digital prize pack, including a free book!

WHAT'S NEXT?

It all started when a vengeful seagull with a shady past promised to wage a brutal war against my wedding day. Things snowballed pretty quickly from there.

I always thought my special day would be perfect. Now, all I want is to get through it without any major catastrophes.

And that's pretty hard with four hyped-up cats running underfoot—two who are so desperately in love it makes you want to puke, and two more who very much don't want me as their new stepmother and aren't afraid to tell me so... constantly.

By the time a certain friend shows up with the film crew for her floundering reality TV in tow, I know I'm in big trouble.

Not only could I fail to make it down the aisle, but I also risk exposing my biggest, most intimate secret.

So when all is finally said and done, will I be saying "I do" to the man of my dreams or admitting "I can" when forced to confess to my Pet Whisperer abilities?

SCHEMING SPHYNX is now available.

Get your copy so that you can keep reading this zany mystery series today!

SNEAK PEEK

SCHEMING SPHYNX

My name is Angie Russo, and in just a few short days, I will become Mrs. Charles Longfellow, III. It seems like ages since that first day our eyes met across the office and I instantly fell head over heels for the handsome new law associate from California. Really though, it's only been a couple years.

And even though I immediately fell in love, it took Charles a little longer to figure out I was the one he'd spend the rest of his life with. It all started when he blackmailed me into helping with a difficult double homicide case. He was the second person to learn of my strange ability to talk to animals, and rather than gawk at me, he decided to put me to work.

Now we've solved many cases, both together

and apart, and in the process we've fallen irrevo-
cably in love. He's now the sole partner at the firm,
and I've moved on from paralegalling to working as
a full-time private investigator... in theory.

In reality, I primarily live off my cat's trust fund,
but I do try my best to find new mysteries to solve,
whether or not my help has been requested. Why,
just this spring, I solved the murder of my next-
door neighbor. Oh, was that one a doozy!

Luckily, we've been light on work in the weeks
that followed, giving me plenty of time to focus on
wedding planning.

So, that's me. Former paralegal, current private
investigator, future bride. And oh, you wanted to
know more about the whole talking to animals
thing?

Well, it all started when I met Octo-Cat at a
rather unusual will reading. This was before
Charles had even joined the firm. He was the first
one to really trust me to help research our cases.
Before that, I was mostly a glorified secretary. And
that day, it was my job to make the coffee. Things
didn't exactly go well, and let's just say I've had a
completely rational fear of that particular appliance
ever since.

The unexpected zap messed with something in

my brain, and when I regained consciousness, I was met with big amber eyes and stinky tuna breath. Yes, the estate's primary beneficiary was a cat, and when he realized I could understand everything he was saying, he recruited me to help solve his owner's murder.

And thus a lifelong *something* was born. Most days Octo-Cat and I get along fine, but sometimes he can be a real stinker. Still, I wouldn't trade him —or really any part of my life—for the world.

My true best friend is my nan. She's the main one who raised me while my parents focused on making the most of their careers. She's not even my biological grandmother, a fact I discovered only quite recently. And after months of searching and with a little help from a militant flock of seagulls, I was recently able to meet my Grandma Lyn—the one who gave birth to Mom.

Both will be at the wedding, which will definitely be awkward. But we'll have lots of other guests to help keep the two mostly apart.

Nan's dog Paisley, a mostly black tricolor Chihuahua she rescued from the pound, is going to be the flower girl at our wedding. Pringle, the raccoon who lives in a treehouse in my backyard, is not invited but will probably crash the party anyway. Our seagull friends Bravo and Abigull have told us they'll be watching from the trees. Another seagull I know, Alpha, has threatened to ruin the whole affair. He's also recently befriended Pringle and encouraged him to take part in a twelve-step program to help with his behavioral issues. I'm not sure I trust his motives on that one, but the group therapy has definitely been helping Pringle to turn over a new leaf.

He's still not invited to the wedding, though.

I'll be plenty busy hosting all the guests we have coming from out of town. Even my old frenemy Bethany Peters is coming up from Georgia along with my cousin Mags to take part in the happiest day of my life to date.

Charles's family is coming out from California, of course, and our friend Sharon is taking a detour on her RV tour of the country to swing on by too. Basically, everyone who's anyone to us will be in attendance—past clients, old friends, distant family... Even my cat's girlfriend's owner is coming all the way from Colorado to pay her respects.

In lieu of a bridal party, our three cats will be standing at the altar with us. I've found adorable bowties for Octo-Cat and Jacques and a miniature lace veil for Jillianne. Charles hasn't been owned by cats as long as I have, but he's a sucker for the two hairless Sphynx he inherited from my first dead next-door neighbor, Senator Harlowe.

Over the last several months, I've been giving the two speech lessons to help them overcome their strange accents—not out of the goodness of my heart, but rather at Octo-Cat's demand. He made it very clear that neither Charles nor his cats would be welcome in our house unless the two kittyfolk stopped communicating in only riddles and rhymes.

It was a tall order, but I'm fairly accustomed to my cat bossing me around, and this demand wasn't particularly unreasonable as far as Octo-Cat goes, which meant I was happy to comply. Plus it gave me a chance to bond with Jacques and Jillianne ahead of us becoming one big happy family.

They weren't too sure about me at first, but now I'm fairly certain I've won them over...

SCHEMING SPHYNX is now available.

Get your copy so that you can keep reading this zany mystery series today!

ABOUT MOLLY FITZ

While *USA Today bestselling* author Molly Fitz can't technically talk to animals, she and her three feline writing assistants have deep and very animated conversations as they navigate their days.

She lives with her child and their own private zoo somewhere in the wilds of Alaska. Molly will occasionally venture out for good food, great coffee, or to meet new animal friends.

Learn more about Molly and her books, and be sure to sign up for her newsletter at **www.Molly Mysteries.com**.

ALSO BY MOLLY FITZ

Learn more about Molly's collected works, so that you can decide which book you'd like to read next...

PET WHISPERER P.I.

Angie Russo just partnered up with Blueberry Bay's first ever talking cat detective. Along with his ragtag gang of human and animal helpers, Octo-Cat is determined to save the day... so long as it doesn't interfere with his schedule.

Start with book 1, ***Kitty Confidential***.

MERLIN'S MAGICAL MYSTERIES

Gracie Springs is not a witch... but her cat is. Now she must help to keep his secret or risk spending the rest of her life in some magical prison. Too bad trouble seems to find them at every turn!

Start with book 1, ***Merlin Takes a Familiar***.

PARANORMAL TEMP AGENCY

Tawny Bigford's simple life takes a turn for the magical when she stumbles upon her landlady's murder and is recruited by a talking black cat named Fluffikins to take over the deceased's role as the official Town Witch for Beech Grove, Georgia.

Start with book 1, ***Witch for Hire***.

THE MYSTERIES OF MOONLIGHT MANOR (WITH TRIXIE SILVERTALE)

Sydney Coleman has it all—until she doesn't. No sooner does she launch her bed and breakfast, than a trio of ghosts turn up oppose her at every turn. They insist she solve the murder of their mistress, but Sydney is desperate for cash. If she can't book some guests fast, her haunted mansion is utterly doomed.

Start with book 1, ***Moonlight & Mischief***.

CONNECT WITH MOLLY

Sign up for my newsletter and get a special digital prize pack for joining, including an exclusive story, *Meowy Christmas Mayhem*, fun quiz, and lots of cat pictures!

Sign up: **MollyMysteries.com/subscribe**

Now, if you ever wished you could converse with cats, here's your opportunity! This is me officially inviting you into my whacky inner world as part of my Cozy Kitty Book Club.

For those who just can't get enough of my zany cat characters and their hapless humans, this book club will provide new content to devour and the chance to get to know my best author friends.

From exclusive stories, behind-the-scenes trivia to never-before-released bonus content, and monthly giveaways, there's a lot to love about the Cozy Kitty Book Club. Join today to find out what we're reading next!

Join: **MollyMysteries.com/club**